The Single Mom Diaries

First comes baby, then comes happily-ever-after

The Darling sisters, both single moms, have always supported each other through the ups and downs of life and love. But they'll need each other's advice more than ever when the possibility of true love comes knocking!

Playboy Connor McNair thinks life behind a picket fence isn't his speed—until Jill Darling, the girl he secretly loves, traps him with kisses and Bundt cake. How can he turn away from the woman he's always wanted and her twin baby boys?

Don't miss

A DADDY FOR HER SONS

April 2013

Sara Darling's joy at adopting her deceased half sister's baby turns into a bad dream when she realizes that the rough, handsome man she's just met has come to claim that same child. Could a marriage of convenience with Sara be exactly the medicine that tortured Jake Martin needs?

Find out in

MARRIAGE FOR HER BABY

June 2013

Dear Reader,

Sara Darling, the heroine of this story, is renovating her house on the beach. I love to give my characters a house on the beach—because that's what I've always dreamed of having.

Can you imagine? The sound of the waves creating the background music to your daily life. The sun breaking out and lighting up your afternoon. The foghorns late at night as fog wraps around your house like a blanket, hiding you from the rest of the world.

When you're upset you can go out and walk in the sand to think it through, now and then letting the water lap at your ankles. When you're happy—a picnic or a late-night bonfire. In the morning you walk to the local village and stop for a cup of coffee at the little sidewalk café. In the evening you walk to your favorite little restaurant for dinner.

Heaven on earth! At least in my imagination.

Oh, I know reality isn't quite so idyllic—not when you factor in the weekends and summer days when the tourists take all your parking places and camp out in your front yard, fill the restaurants with screaming children, and drop their sticky drinks and ice cream cones in your driveway.

So instead of living at the beach, I'm just one of those tourists.

Oops—sorry, beach house people!

Thanks to all of you who read my books. I love you!

Raye Morgan

RAYE MORGAN

Marriage for Her Baby

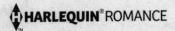
HARLEQUIN®ROMANCE

Recycling programs
for this product may
not exist in your area.

ISBN-13: 978-0-373-74245-5

MARRIAGE FOR HER BABY

First North American Publication 2013

Copyright © 2013 by Helen Conrad

For questions and comments about the quality of this book,
please contact us at CustomerService@Harlequin.com.

® and TM are trademarks of Harlequin Enterprises Limited or its
corporate affiliates. Trademarks indicated with ® are registered in the
United States Patent and Trademark Office, the Canadian Trade Marks
Office and in other countries.

Printed in U.S.A.

HARLEQUIN®
www.Harlequin.com

Raye Morgan has been a nursery school teacher, a travel agent, a clerk and a business editor, but her best job ever has been writing romances—and fostering romance in her own family at the same time. Current score: two boys married, two more to go. Raye has published more than seventy romance novels and claims to have many more waiting in the wings. She lives in Southern California with her husband and whichever son happens to be staying at home at the moment.

Recent books by Raye Morgan:

Other titles by this author available in ebook format.

To Patience Bloom, aptly named and endowed with talents for perception, encouragement and support that go above and beyond every day!

CHAPTER ONE

SARA DARLING WAS collecting donations for the Children's Sunshine Fund throughout her bayside neighborhood, and it wasn't easy over the last weeks of summer when everyone was gone on vacation. The beach was unusually warm today and the stairs to each cottage seemed higher and higher as she moved down the beachfront area. To make that climb and then come up with no answer to her knock was demoralizing. The only people who opened the doors were vacation renters, and they weren't interested in donating to a local fund.

"Collecting," she muttered sarcastically as fat beads of sweat began a race down her spine. "Begging would be a better name for it."

Somehow she let her sister Jill talk her into

doing this every year, and every year, she swore it would be the last time. She walked past her own little house and smiled. She hadn't been living in it for the last few weeks. Renovations were underway. She could hardly wait to go in and see it all changed. Just a few more days and work should be over. She could pack up her baby and move back home.

The last house on her schedule was the one next to hers. The neighbors were in Europe on their annual trek, but they did rent out to short-term vacationers. She looked at the red door and sighed, wishing she could head back to her baby right now. One last climb.

She made it and gave a short knock on the door. No response. Oh, well. She started to turn away, but a sound from inside turned her back again. What was that? A siren? An alarm? Or was the tenant playing some sort of weird music?

What the heck, it was none of her business. She started to turn away again, but the door suddenly swung open as though someone had yanked it from behind. Sara found herself staring into a pair of icy-blue eyes beneath dark, intimidating brows.

"Yes?" the man asked shortly, as though she was already late answering him.

Unaccountably she was flustered and for a moment, she couldn't remember why she'd come. "I…uh…"

Maybe it was because he was so darn handsome. Or maybe it was because he was looking so fierce. Possibly also in the brew was the fact that his naked torso was muscular and manly and altogether breathtaking, and the way his jeans hung on his hips was enough to give a girl ideas. That might have been a contributing factor. But whatever the cause, her mind was completely blank.

"Hey, you're a woman," he announced gruffly, as though it was something of a revelation to him.

She tried to smile. "So I've been told," she said, attempting light humor that crumbled and died before the words even left her lips.

His frown grew fiercer. "I need a woman. Maybe you can help me. Come on." Reaching out, he grabbed her wrist and pulled her into the house, letting the door slam behind her.

"Wait a minute!"

"No time. All hell is breaking loose. Come on. Quickly."

Truth be told, she was pretty sure she would have resisted with a bit more spunk if it hadn't been for the oddly disturbing noises coming from the very room they were dashing toward. Curiosity was strong here, and it was rewarded. He threw open the double doors and ushered her into a little piece of madness.

The noise was overwhelming. Something was rotating and banging against the wall. Some form of food sizzled and spit on the stove, and thick waves of suds poured out of the dishwasher. A cat had climbed halfway up the inside of the screen door and was howling for escape. The refrigerator door stood open, creating an annoying electronic warning buzz. Meanwhile cans of soda were slowly rolling out and hitting the floor. Now and then, one burst open and shot carbonated beverage across the walls. A cloud of black smoke was emanating from the toaster and the smell of burning bread was in the air.

"You see what I mean?" the man shouted above the din. "Where do I start?"

Whatever was sizzling on the stove suddenly burst into tall orange flames, which shot toward the ceiling. She gaped. The gates of hell might have looked something like this.

Sara took it all in and suppressed the scream of horror that wanted to push its way up her throat. This was no time to panic. She had to be cool, calm, collected.

But she wasn't perfect. "Oh, my goodness… what?" she cried, knowing there was going to be no answer until disaster had been headed off at the pass. "Are you crazy?"

He spread out his hands and shook his head. "Help," he said.

She looked at him. He was actually waiting for her to tell him what to do. She gulped. He wasn't the type. She knew that instinctively. But here he was, asking for assistance—from her. Help indeed!

She pushed back the panic and tried to think clearly. Wait. She knew all these items intimately. The situations, taken one at a time, were all things she'd dealt with before. Darn it all, she could handle this. Suddenly she realized it was true. She could take command. Why not? He was obviously clueless.

She grabbed his arm. "Okay," she shouted

in order to be heard above the din. "Turn off the dishwasher. I'll take care of the fire."

He turned to look at it. The flames appeared fiery, leaping higher every minute. "You will?" he said doubtfully.

She didn't waste any more time. The lid to the frying pan was lying on the floor. She reached down to grab it, took a deep breath and plunged forward, firmly slamming it down on the pan, smothering the flames almost instantly. Quickly turning the knob for the gas, she doused its fuel. And then she took a deep breath of relief.

"Hey," he said, looking impressed.

"The dishwasher," she reminded him, jerking her head in that direction. They were going to be swimming in suds in no time if he didn't stop the flow. She could just picture the two of them waltzing across the slippery floor and landing on their backsides.

"Right," he said. He actually looked like he knew what he was doing so she headed for the washing machine at the far end of the kitchen. It was doing a spin cycle, but it was unbalanced and creating a terrible noise as it bounced around. Reaching out with a strange new confidence, she snapped off the juice. Like a crazed windup toy coming back to sanity, it began to wind down its banging cascade.

"How do I turn this thing off?" he was calling to her as he peered at the knobs and buttons on the dishwasher.

So she'd been wrong. He had no idea what he was doing. But wasn't that obvious by now? She strode over and slapped the off switch as she passed, never missing a beat, on her way to the refrigerator. There, she caught the last two cans before they hit the floor, unended them, placed them on a shelf and closed the door.

The awful noise from the washing machine had stopped. The sizzle was dying down in the frying pan. The refrigerator alarm had faded away and the suds were slowing down.

She looked at the toaster. A black cloud still hovered over it, but nothing new was burning. At least he seemed to have unplugged it on his own, so that was taking care of itself by now.

However, the smoke alarm it had probably triggered was shouting a warning over and over. "Evacuate! Evacuate! There is smoke in the basement. Evacuate!"

She looked at him for an explanation and he shook his head. "There is no basement," he told her. "The thing's gone crazy."

"How do you turn it off?" she asked him, knowing there had to be a way and knowing at the same time that he wasn't going to know what that was.

"You got me."

She hesitated. It was up so high, she couldn't fan it with a towel like she usually did with hers. But something had to be done. It was getting louder and louder, as if it were angry they weren't paying enough attention. She looked around the room and saw a broom. Grabbing it, she placed it in his hand.

"Kill it," she said.

He almost laughed. "You're kidding."

She shook her head. She was feeling a little wild. "You're taller. Swing at it with the brush end of the broom. That might do it. If not, do you have a gun?"

He did laugh this time, but he swung at it, forcing air into its core and finally, like a gift, it stopped yelling.

"Oh, my gosh," she said, sagging against the counter. "What a relief."

"Almost done," he said, turning to look at the cat that was still clinging to the screen door and howling at the top of its lungs.

"Is he your cat?" she asked, looking at the poor terrified thing with its claws stuck.

He shook his head. "Never saw him before in my life. He must have been hiding in here when it all began."

She nodded. She'd thought as much. She'd seen him around the neighborhood for ages.

"Okay. You're going to have to help me. This is going to be a two-part play."

He nodded, watching her. "Just tell me what to do."

She glanced into his eyes, expecting a touch of ridicule. He was the sort of man she would have thought would be ready to put her back in her place by now. But, no. His eyes were clear and ready. He really was waiting for her to tell him what to do.

For some reason, that made her heart beat faster. She scanned the room. "We'll need a towel," she said.

He turned and grabbed one from a pile of

dirty clothes in front of the washer. It looked as though he'd just emptied a duffel bag right there. He handed her the towel and she regarded the cat. The only way she'd ever managed to take her cat—when she had one—to the veterinarian was by wrapping him firmly so that no claws were exposed. But that was a cat who knew and loved her. This one was a stranger. She only hoped she didn't end up a bloody mess when this was over and done.

"Okay. I'll grab him. You whip open the door."

"It opens to a back porch," he warned her. "You want me to go all the way through that and open a door to the backyard?"

"Absolutely," she said, nodding. "Okay, here goes."

She drew in a deep, deep breath, muttered a little prayer and lunged for the cat. He saw her coming and yelled a threat, a deep, vibrant howl. If he'd been free to fly, he would have done it, but luckily his claws were stuck just enough so that he couldn't move.

The next part was tricky. She had to get him wrapped really well and do it fast, but at the same time, she didn't want to hurt him and his claws being stuck shifted from being an advantage to being a problem. She threw the towel around and hugged him, lifting slightly to loosen his claws. Somehow it worked out fine. Only a few claws continued to stick, and then only for a few seconds. As he came loose, she wrapped his paws quickly and clamped down tight. He howled and struggled but she gritted her teeth and held on, carrying him quickly out as the man opened the doors for her.

The cat was strong and he'd almost worked his way out of the towel by the time she hit the backyard and she didn't get to put him down as gently as she would have liked. But she hardly saw him at all. In a flash, he was gone. She looked around and tried to catch her breath. Then she turned and saw the man staring at her in wonder.

"Wow," he said. "You're incredible."

She stared back at him, surprised. He meant it. But she thought about it for a second. She sort of was, wasn't she? She'd handled all this pretty well, if she did say so herself. Now that things had calmed down, she couldn't believe that she'd been able to maintain that sort of control. She'd moved smoothly, with purpose and determination.

That really wasn't much like her. Hey. She was pretty proud of herself.

As for him…well, what on earth was that all about, anyway? She shook her head.

"How could you get so many things wrong at one time?" she asked, still amazed at what they'd just experienced.

He gave her a crooked grin that didn't seem to reach his eyes. "Pretty amazing, isn't it? I don't know. I just seem to have a talent for failure lately."

"I doubt that." She rejected his explanation out of hand. No, he had the look and feel of a man who did just about everything right. Only—today things had spun out of control for a bit. Interesting.

They were standing in the backyard and neither of them seemed to have any interest in going back into the kitchen. She shuddered when she thought of it.

"Seriously," he said. "I've spent most of my time living in hotel rooms or tents over the last few years. I've lost the knack of civilization."

She wanted to laugh but he wasn't even smiling. "Surely you didn't grow up in a cave," she said.

"No." He raised his bright blue eyes to meet hers. "It was more of a hut. And after my mother died, we didn't live much like modern people do. My father caught game and fished and we lived off that. People called us the Wild Ones in my town. I resented it at the time, but looking back, I guess we deserved it."

She couldn't look away from his brilliant blue gaze. He had her mesmerized. She could see him living rough, like a twentieth century native. All he needed was a horse and a blanket and off he would go.

But the twentieth century was over and the modern world wasn't very open to living like a wild one. Very deliberately, she took a step backward, as if she could somehow make a move out of his sphere of suggestive influence by putting more space between them. It didn't work, and she found herself smoothing back her sleek blond hair like a woman primping for an encounter.

Ouch!

She wasn't going to do that. She was so far from being in the market for a flirtation, she hardly remembered what that would be like. She finally pulled her gaze away and shook her head.

"You've got a lot of cleaning up to do in there," she noted.

"Not me," he said decisively.

She frowned at him. "You can't just leave it. You're going to have to clean it sometime."

"Are you kidding?" His sudden grin was a revelation. "I'm not going back in there."

She gasped. "But…"

"I'll just go and rent a new place and start over, armed with all I've learned from you."

It took a moment to realize he was kidding. She shook her head, not sure what to make of him.

He was tall and hard and strong with a body that could have been chiseled from Carrara marble. That's what he reminded her of—the gang at the Parthenon. A Greek god for heaven's sake—with a face to match. His features were crisp and even—handsome in a hard, rough way. His eyes with their long, dark lashes had a sleepy, languorous expression. Very appealing.

But was there any warmth there? If there was, she couldn't find it. Was he as cold as marble, too? All in all, he was gorgeous, but he was also a little bit scary.

He watched her with one dark eyebrow raised.

"Tell you what, let's go down to the corner café. I'll buy you a cup of coffee."

That startled her. She'd sworn off men a long time ago. The aggravation wasn't worth the reward. She had other things in her life, things she valued. Besides, he might be a short-term renter in the house next to hers, but that didn't mean they were destined to be bosom buddies. Not at all. She took his offer as a cue to begin to back away.

"Oh, I don't know, I've got to…"

"Come on." He touched her. It was just a gesture, just a quick, passing touch. He probably didn't even notice when his fingertips softly slipped along her arm. But she did. It gave her a start and her breath was suddenly catching in her throat.

"Come on. I owe you one. You just did me a very big favor."

"Well…" She was weakening. A part of her stood aside and watched this with exasperation. What on earth was she doing? But she snuck a look at her watch and realized she actually had plenty of time. She knew her baby would still be napping at her sister's house for another half hour, at least. So…why not?

She glanced at him sideways. "Just for a few minutes," she conceded.

"Good," he said, sticking his hand out. "I'm Jake Martin. And I would guess that your name is Jill."

"Oh, no." She shook her head, wondering how he'd come up with her sister's name, then she realized she was wearing Jill's uniform shirt for doing the Sunshine Fund collecting. "Jill" was embroidered in big red letters right over the pocket. She laughed. "No, actually…"

"Come on, Jill," he said, taking her hand. "Let's go."

Her heart seemed to roll over inside her. She glanced at his muscular chest and knew she was turning bright red.

"You're going to need a shirt, aren't you?" she noted breathlessly.

"Oh." He stopped short and looked down at his lack of attire. "Hey, sorry. I hadn't realized I was being so informal. I'll grab something out of my car."

He turned to do just that and she gasped softly as she noticed the purple scarring on his back, a picture of past pain and agony she hadn't noticed before in all the commotion. She turned away and pretended not to watch as he pulled a dark blue T-shirt over that beautiful body.

"Listen, I left my papers and my purse in your house. I'm going to have to go in to get them."

He groaned. "Okay. But I don't want to see it. I'll meet you out front."

She made her way quickly through the mess, glad it wasn't going to be her job to clean it up, grabbed her things and came out the front door to meet him. He smiled and took hold of her hand again and they were marching toward the coffee shop.

"I really like it here," he told her, looking out at the gray-blue ocean that surrounded the Washington State island just across from Seattle where they lived—for the moment at least.

She liked it, too. In fact she planned to spend a long, long time here. That was why she was renovating her house to make room for raising Savannah, her nine-month-old baby.

A group of seagulls flew overhead, screaming in their usual argument. She looked down toward the other end of town. The ferry was coming in, bringing commuters home from their jobs in Seattle. Yes, this was where she wanted to be.

"Too bad I can't stay," Jake said, looking like he really did regret it.

"Where are you going instead?" she asked, just to make conversation.

He hesitated. "I'm not sure," he told her, staring right down into her eyes. "I haven't had time to think it through. But it will be somewhere different." His smile was crooked. "It always is."

She could see that he was telling her the truth. But he was outside his comfort zone at the moment. She wondered why.

They went into the little café and took a booth, sitting across from each other. Coffee, he'd said, and she wasn't hungry, but she picked up the menu and began to peruse it, just to give herself something to do besides stare at him.

"You said you'd been living in a tent lately," she reminded him, peeking around the menu. "What was that all about?"

"I've been in the military," he said shortly, looking away as though it was something he didn't want to talk about.

"As if that wasn't obvious," she muttered, glancing back at the menu.

"Why?" he said.

She shrugged. "There's a military look about you," she said.

He frowned and she looked away again. So he didn't like the fact that she could see his military influence. Too bad. It was only obvious and she could have said more.

She could have mentioned that he had a noticeable restlessness in him, a sort of masculine urge to gaze at the horizon and wonder what might be out there. It was the sort of thing that made most women sigh with regret.

He wasn't the sort to be tied down by anyone. It was written all over him. You fell for a man like this and you were playing with fire.

"Iced tea, please," she asked as the waitress stood poised, pad of paper in hand.

"Coffee for me," he said. "Black. And two pieces of cherry pie. Á la mode."

She looked at him and held back her smile. "You must be really hungry," she said.

"No. But I can see that you are," he shot back. Then he grinned and that took all the sting out of it. "You'll love the pie here," he said. "Trust me."

Trust him. That was just what she was having a bit of problem doing. And where did he get off telling her what the pie was like in her own little café? That did it. She'd known she should have rejected his offer from the first. The man was obviously insufferable.

But he was also right. The pie was great. She looked around the restaurant, surprised she didn't see anyone she knew. Only the girl behind the counter seemed familiar at all. But she usually stopped by for a large cup of coffee in the morning, and the crew in the afternoon were mostly different. It was odd to be in a place that was so familiar, and yet feel like a stranger.

Odd, but not unusual for her. She hadn't made many friends since she'd moved to the island, and the ones she did know didn't really know much about her. She kept things to herself.

And there was a secret about her that not even most of the people closest to her knew. She'd never been in love.

She'd been in pretty heavy-duty "like" a time or two. She'd known some very nice men and she'd had relationships. She'd even been engaged once. But somehow she'd always felt a little bit apart, as though she were an observer of her own talent at romance—and marking herself down critically every time.

Her engagement had been a high point. She'd really liked Freddy. He was fun and good-natured and liked to do many of the things she liked. His family was so nice. She could just see the trajectory of the life they would have together and it followed exactly what she would have expected for herself. It all fit. Why not? Why not go ahead and marry him and hope that it would all work out?

She became obsessed with pretending that she was in love. She tried so hard. But when he hugged her, she found herself craning to see what time it was. When he told her of his life plans, she found herself daydreaming instead of throwing herself into his ambitions the way she should have. And when he kissed her, there was no sparkle.

She told herself not to be so childish. Who the heck needed sparkle? And then she realized—she did. Just a little. Was that asking too much?

When they split up, she felt nothing but relief, and since then, she'd hardly given their relationship another thought. Looking back, she knew now that there had been very little love involved on either of their parts. There had been a longing for a regular, ordinary life, but it had very little to do with any strong emotional tie between them.

She just didn't seem to have what it took to create a loving relationship, and she'd resigned herself to concentrating on her career. Now there was something she was good at.

She had finished half her piece of pie and was trying to decide if she was going to eat the rest. It was awfully good, but the calories! She'd always been on the slender side, but that fit figure wasn't easy to keep that way. Pushing the plate away, she looked up at Jake instead.

"So you were telling me about living in a tent," she reminded him.

"Was I?"

"Yes. And then you got annoyed when I said I could tell you were military." She smiled. She was nothing if not helpful.

He gave her a disbelieving glance, but he willingly picked up the thread and went on. "I've been deployed mostly to Southeast Asia for the last couple of years," he filled in. "We did a lot of living off the land. Subsisting on roadkill and taro root."

She made a face. She didn't know whether to take him seriously or not, but the humorous glint in his eyes was a pretty big hint. "Don't they give you guys C rations anymore?" she asked tartly.

He leaned back and looked at her through heavy lidded eyes. "Now that would be giving away the military connection from the get-go, don't you think?" he drawled.

She narrowed her eyes, refusing to let him intimidate her. "So you were working under-cover, were you?" she said, pleased with her-self for making the connection.

But his eyes turned a stormy-gray. "Not lately," he said shortly. "I was doing some time in a terrorist prison camp—as a detainee. And believe me, we were happy to get taro root. It was the fat, squishy insects that made you gag."

She gazed at him, not sure if he was still pulling the wool over her eyes or not. He seemed awfully serious. She decided to play along, regardless. "So that was why you said you had forgotten how to live like a civilized person?"

He nodded. "I felt I needed to get back in the groove. So I decided to try out all the mod-ern conveniences I hadn't ever used before, all at once." His quick grin was self-deprecat-ing and it left as suddenly as it had appeared. "Like I thought I could get the learning curve over with faster that way. As you can see, it didn't work very well."

"Okay," she told him sensibly. "So start

over, only this time do one thing a day until you've mastered it."

He was shaking his head. "No time," he said. "I've got to learn fast. I'm going to need it all very soon."

She smiled. "Because you rented a nice little house with appliances?"

He didn't smile back. "No. Something more important than that."

She waited for a moment, but he didn't elaborate. She couldn't imagine what it might be, but she was curious. In fact, she was becoming more and more interested in this gorgeous, compelling man. There was no use trying to pretend. For the first time in years, she'd met a man who not only made her pulse dance, but made her think warm thoughts of all kinds.

Ordinarily that would make her back away and find an excuse to be somewhere else. But she couldn't do that with Jake Martin. She was starting to wish she could think of a reason to ask him over for dinner.

Wait. She had the perfect reason.

His house had practically exploded that afternoon. He couldn't go back there until something was done about the mess. So she wouldn't feel hesitant about asking him over—even if it was to her sister's house. She smiled again and waited for a chance to get an invitation in.

But meanwhile, there was the question of that important thing that made him want to learn how to run a house.

"Am I supposed to guess what it is?" she asked.

She was almost flirting now. Maybe she ought to hold that back for the time being. She'd forgotten how much fun it could be— that little surge of electricity as your eyes met his—that little bobble of excitement in your chest. Flirting. She was going to have to work on it a bit, but it could be an asset. She bit her lower lip and waited for an answer.

"No, of course not," he said, his blue eyes sparkling. "Sorry to be so secretive, but there are reasons."

"Go ahead," she said recklessly. "You can tell me anything."

He hesitated, looking at her as though trying to decide if he could trust her.

She smiled, trying to look trustworthy.

He shrugged. "Okay, I'll tell you why." He

leaned forward so that he could speak more confidentially. "I'm about to become a father. And I've got to learn how to take care of my little girl as quickly as I can."

CHAPTER TWO

Sara gazed at Jake, amazed. A little girl—just like Savannah. Funny how similar their stories seemed to be. Maybe he was adopting his little girl, the same way she was adopting hers. Or maybe—she glanced at his hand, looking for a ring and he noted her interest with a crooked grin.

"No, I'm not married," he said. "But I do have a little girl and in a few days, she'll be with me. I've got to be ready to take care of her. I've got to learn all this stuff."

"Of course you do."

She smiled at him. Finally there was a flicker of warmth in his eyes and it had to be because he was talking about his baby. She knew the feeling. She'd considered herself a career woman for years until Savannah had come into her life. And now her entire reality was totally focused on that child.

She leaned forward, wanting to know all about it but not wanting to seem too nosy. She thought of her own nine-month-old baby, and her smile widened. He was in for such joy if his experience was even half as rewarding as hers had been.

Savannah had been the child of her younger half sister. After Kelly died in a car accident, Sara had volunteered to take her. She'd been reluctant at first. She and her sister Jill hadn't had any contact with Kelly for a long time and knew nothing about her baby. Besides, Sara was about to make a major step forward in her career, a job that would take all her time.

But in the end, the baby came first.

Now she couldn't even remember that struggle to decide very clearly. Her very existence revolved around this baby she'd only had for less than six months. She couldn't imagine life without her. In just a few minutes she would get a chance to tell Jake all about her. The anticipation made her smile.

"I've always been a quick study in my line of work," Jake said. "And since I didn't know anything, I decided the best thing to do would be to just start teaching myself how to cook and to clean and all the rest. Just go ahead and jump in with both feet. So today was the day." He threw his head back and groaned. "Disaster."

She had to admit that was pretty accurate. "Think of it as a learning experience," she told him. "I think you need more planning ahead of time. And maybe lessons would help."

"Lessons." He nodded, thinking that over. "Maybe you could teach me a few more tricks?" He looked at her, his face endearingly pathetic.

"Why not?"

That was her first, exuberant reaction, but it only took seconds to make her wonder what the heck she thought she was getting into. Her interior watchdog was yelling, "No, no, no, no!" That was exactly what she'd programmed it to do if she was ever in danger of falling for a man again. But she was very tempted to ignore it. Maybe her luck had changed. How would she ever know if she didn't try?

"So tell me about your little girl," she said, wondering if it would be a good time to ask him what his dinner plans were. Maybe not.

Better wait another ten minutes or so. "How old is she? When did you see her last?"

He frowned. "I think she's about nine months old," he said. "I think that's what they told me."

Nine months. That was the same as Savannah. "You're adopting her?" Sara asked.

But he shook his head. "No. She's mine. I just didn't know about her until I got released from the camp and sent home to the States."

Somewhere deep inside, very near her heart, a new warning was beginning to send a small, nervous signal to her brain. She touched her breastbone with her fingers, gently pushing as though she could push the feeling back. But it just got stronger. Something wasn't quite right here.

But that was silly. She had no real reason to think that at all. He was telling her the facts as he knew them—why would that be threatening? She was being ridiculous. Probably because she wasn't used to talking to men like this.

"What's your baby's name?"

He shook his head. "Funny thing is, they

never told me that. I guess I'll be able to name her whatever I want."

"So you've never seen her?"

"No." His smile was brilliant. "But I've seen pictures, and she's a beauty—a little blonde with dark eyes and the biggest smile I've ever seen."

Sara was feeling sick. She wasn't sure why. But something was beginning to feel very wrong. Why did everything he said seem to have such a close resemblance to her Savannah?

Stop it, she told herself. *That's crazy. What he is describing is the picture of almost any little nine-month-old girl. Don't let your imagination carry you away. Just stop it!*

"What happened to her mother?" she asked, surprised to hear how raspy her voice sounded.

He shook his head. "She's out of the picture," was all he said.

What did that mean? That she didn't want the child? That she didn't want a relationship with Jake? That she was an unfit mother and he had to take over? It could mean a thousand things. It could also mean—no, she didn't want to go there.

"So they've told you that your baby is all yours?" she asked, feeling breathless. "Are you taking possession of her here? Or…?"

He grimaced. "Actually I'm not supposed to be here yet. I found out where she's staying and I came to get as close to her as I could. I want to be ready to go, as soon as the paperwork is all taken care of. We've just got to tie up a few loose ends, and I'll be taking custody of her."

As close to her as he could. Yeah, next door was pretty close. Pure, cold, electric panic was beginning to shiver through her system. It couldn't be. Could it?

"You said the mother is out of the picture," she repeated. Her voice sounded so strange and her mouth was so dry. "Permanently?"

He looked at her curiously, as though wondering why she cared. "Yes. She died in a car accident."

"Oh. I'm so sorry." Her words came automatically, but her hand rose and covered her mouth. Inside, she was screaming.

"Me, too." He shrugged. "But I really didn't know her very well. And now I've found she left me this wonderful gift." He shook his head. "Life is crazy, isn't it?"

"Yes."

She had to go. She had to get out of here. Maybe she was taking this completely wrong, but there were too many things that seemed to lead right to her situation—to her baby. *It couldn't be. Oh, please, don't let it be...*

She began to gather her clipboard and purse, preparing to make her escape.

"You know the neighborhood pretty well, don't you?" he was asking.

What? She blinked at him. It was almost as though he was speaking a foreign language. But she took a deep breath and forced herself to settle down and translate to her frightened mind.

"I...I've lived here for three years, but I traveled a lot on business. So, no, I guess I can't claim to know the neighborhood really well. Why?"

"I was just wondering if you knew a woman named Sara Darling."

There it was—as though a huge gong of doom had been rung in her head. It was still ringing, echoing back and forth, deafening her. This was it. Everything she'd been dreading was coming down on her and she had to go. She began to tremble uncontrollably. She looked around, ready to run.

But at the same time, she couldn't give it all away. She couldn't let him know. She needed time to get away. So she tried to smile.

"Sara Darling?" Sara could hardly get the name out of her dry mouth. "I, uh, well, no, I…"

Ordinarily she would be laughing and explaining how he'd had her name wrong from the beginning, and that she was Sara Darling herself. But that didn't happen. She couldn't let him know who she really was. The shock of his question had pierced her heart and it was going to take some time to right herself again.

"She's supposed to be living next door to the house I rented," he went on, "but I've been there for two days and I haven't seen a sign of her."

"Oh." *Calm down, Sara,* she was telling herself. *You've got to make it through this. Calm down.*

She had to go. She had to get out of here.

Her heart was pounding so hard, she was sure he had to hear it.

"Hey, I'm sorry," she said quickly as she slid out of the booth. "I just remembered something I have to do. Thanks so much for the pie. I'll…I'll see you around."

She didn't stop to see how he took her sudden departure. She just went, walking quickly through the tiny café, then breaking into a run as she hit the street.

By the time Sara reached her sister's house at the top of the hill overlooking the ferry landing, she thought her lungs would burst.

"Sara, what is it?" Jill called, seeing her entrance from the kitchen where she was baking. "What on earth is the matter?"

She rushed out to greet her and Sara clung to her, trying to catch her breath.

"Where's Savannah?" she choked out as soon as she could speak.

"In her bed. She's still taking her nap." Jill frowned. "Honey, she's okay. What's wrong?"

"Nothing. I just…nothing."

Jill shrugged, searching her face. "Well, go ahead and check on her, but I just was up there getting the twins ready to go outside and play and she was snoozing away."

Sara nodded and started for the stairs.

"Oh, you had a couple of phone calls," Jill called after her. "One was from the Children's Home Agency. They wanted you to call back right away."

Sara turned to look at her. "Did you write down the number?"

"Of course. It's right by the phone." Jill frowned. "Sara, you don't look good. What's the matter?"

Sara held up her hand. "I'll tell you later. Right now, I've got to call the agency."

"Sure." Jill nodded, though she still looked concerned. "I'll be in the kitchen. I've got an order of Bundt cakes that need to go out by six."

Sara waved her off, turned to the phone and found the paper with the number on it. She dialed it quickly and got through to a real live agent almost immediately.

"We've been trying to get hold of you for the last few days," an agent named Linda told her. "You really must keep in better contact.

If you're going to be away, you must let us know."

"Sorry. I'm sorry. I'll take care of it next time." Sara tried to stop her heart from racing so wildly. "Is there…is there something wrong?"

There was a pause and it nearly killed her. She put her hand over her heart and waited, trying to keep her breathing even.

"Well, I'm afraid something has happened," the woman said at last. "You've been doing so well with your quest to adopt little Savannah."

"My…my sister's child," Sara said, as though that was going to help her win.

"Yes, of course. But you see, there is a problem. Her, uh, her biological father seems to have turned up."

Sara closed her eyes and fought back the urge to vomit. The very thing she'd been afraid of from the beginning now filled her with a terrible dread.

"Are you sure?" she said, her voice raspy, her throat tight. "How can we know he's telling the truth?"

"DNA tests are being performed. We'll know the facts soon enough."

Soon enough. Soon enough. What was the woman talking about?

"But…I've done everything. I've met all the standards. I'm in the process of adopting her right now…."

"You do know that a DNA match will be determinative, don't you? If he can prove that he is her father, well, there's not much we can do."

Sara couldn't speak. She rocked back and forth, holding tightly. Tears were streaming down her face.

"Now don't you give up hope, my dear," the woman was saying. "The DNA might not match. And even if it does, he might decide he is unprepared to take on such a huge responsibility as raising a child on his own. But we do have to come to a conclusion, one way or another, before we can move forward."

"What's his name?" she asked, barely holding herself together.

"His name? Oh. Well, I guess I can tell you that. Jake Martin. He's been away in the military and didn't know that Savannah had been born. Or so he says."

She nodded. She wanted to say more, but she would begin to cry in earnest if she tried.

"I do have to warn you," the voice said, sounding tentative now. "Something happened the last time he was in here. You see, it seems he may have taken a file folder that included your address. It would be completely against regulations to give him your address, of course. But as the file has been missing since his visit…well…I thought you ought to be warned. He might try to contact you."

"Yes," she whispered. "He might." The woman was still talking, but Sara hung up the phone.

She had things to do. She was going to take her baby and run for shelter.

"Be calm," she repeated to herself over and over, breathing in through her nose and out through her mouth. "Remember how you were this afternoon in the crazy kitchen. You can do this. You can make it happen. But you have to stay calm."

They could do it. They would go to a new place and they would hide until the coast was clear, and then… She didn't know what would happen then. But there was no way she was giving up her baby to that...man.

She dashed upstairs and pulled out two travel bags. Working fast, she began to throw clothes into one, baby supplies into the other. They were going to run.

She looked into the crib where Savannah was sleeping. Her beautiful, beautiful baby. For just a moment she filled her heart with the look of her, her round baby cheeks, her perfect eyebrows, her adorable wisp of blond hair. Everything in her ached for this child. To hand her over? To never see her sweet face again? No! She could not, would not—give her up.

And then Jill was in the doorway.

"Sara! What are you doing?"

Sara shook her head and refused to meet her sister's gaze. "Sorry, Jill. We've got to get out of here." She threw some little romper suits into the bag.

Jill grabbed her by the shoulders. "Why? Tell me what's going on."

Sara blinked back tears. "No time."

"Sara!"

"Okay, okay." She took a deep breath. "There's this man who is renting the Lancaster place next to me. His name is Jake Martin. He claims he's Savannah's father."

Jill gasped. "Oh, Sara! No."

"Yes. And he wants her." She set her jaw. "But I won't let him take her. I'm going to go."

"But, Sara, where?"

"Away. As far as we can go. Jill, you do see that I have to do this?"

But Jill was shaking her head. "No," she said softly. "Oh, Sara, no. You can't run. What good will it do? They'll find you. You won't get away. It's too dangerous. Stay here. We'll see what we can do. Maybe Connor will know someone…"

"Jill, he's here. He's looking for her right now. I have to go."

"No!"

"Jill, listen to me. You're the one who talked me into taking this baby. I didn't want to do it. But I saw the light and I did my duty to our sister Kelly. I took her baby. I put all my heart and soul into loving her, caring for her, making her feel cherished and safe. And now you want me to just give her up to some crazy man who doesn't have the slightest idea on how to take care of a child? No. I won't do it. I'm going."

"Wait until Connor gets home," Jill insisted. Pulling out her cell phone, she punched in her husband's number. "Wait. He'll have an idea. I know he will. We can all work on this together."

Sara didn't waste any more time talking. She pulled Savannah into her arms and headed for the changing table. Quickly she changed the diaper as her baby began to wake up and look around, cooing happily as she always did when she saw her mother's face. Sara pulled on a little playsuit and wrapped her in a blanket, then grabbed the suitcases and headed to the door.

She could hear her sister talking to Connor, giving him the facts and urging him to get home fast. But she couldn't wait for that. As she rushed out the door, her main fear was that Jake would already be coming up the hill to Jill's house. She looked quickly, but there was no sign of him, and relief surged in her heart. If she could get to the ferry before he found her, they just might make it. She strapped her baby into the car seat and off they went.

* * *

A good twenty minutes of high anxiety passed
before sanity began to creep back into Sara's
thinking. She was on the ferry by then, parked
behind six cars and in front of two others and
gliding across the water. The wait to board
had seemed to go on forever. She'd sat behind the wheel, scanning the landscape, staring into her rearview mirror, jumping every
time a new man appeared anywhere near.

But he didn't show up. They opened the
gates and let her onto the ferry, and still she
didn't see him anywhere. They started off
across the bay and as time passed, she began
to breathe again. Seattle lay off in the distance. Her thoughts had centered around losing themselves in the big city. As she calmed
down, she began to realize how senseless that
was.

Savannah was fussing a bit and she turned
to reach out for her little hand. She hadn't
thought to bring some snacks for her but she
did have some fresh bottles. Once they got to
the other side, she would pull over in a park
she knew of and take care of that.

Looking at her adorable child, it came to her

in a flash. This was crazy. It was a fantasy—a huge leap out into the great unknown without a safety net. In the modern world there were very few places where you could hide—especially if you were taking a baby with you. You had to have a way to make a living. You had to have someone to watch the baby while you did that. You had to have a place to live in. And all those things required identification. They would be found in no time.

It wouldn't work. She was endangering the welfare of her baby in order to keep control—and losing all control by doing it. This was nuts. Jill had been right. She was going to have to go back.

Her heart sank. She knew it was a sort of defeat. But at the same time, it was only recognizing reality. A thousand things could go wrong, and most of them might hurt Savannah. What had she been thinking? She couldn't risk it.

A sense of doom swept over her, catching in her throat, but she fought it back. There were other ways to fight this. It might take a bit of finesse, a talent for persuasion and a touch for manipulation. But she'd been there before.

Jake Martin wasn't domesticated. He was a wild man. He lived unconventionally. There was nothing in his background or experience that had prepared him to take care of a baby. Surely the powers in the agency would see that. Surely that would go into their decision-making. Or was biology all that mattered?

There was one counselor who had been very helpful to her before, a Mrs. Truesdale. She'd taken a special interest in getting Savannah settled with Sara and had said to call her if there were any problems. That was the one she should have talked to. Maybe she could help.

Her baby's fussing got more insistent.

"Okay, honey," she told her, clicking open her seat belt and opening the car door. "I'm afraid we're going to be turning around and going right back home again. But for now, let's go look at the water. You need some good old ocean wind in your face."

She bundled her baby in the blanket and carried her out onto the deck. A few other passengers were scattered along the railing, watching the icy blue-green water wash by. Lifting her face to the sun, she took a deep breath of fresh air. She was glad they were turning back. She needed to be with her sister. Together, they would think of something. She was sure of it.

She felt the large, hard hand take hold of her upper arm and she didn't have to look to see who it was. But she did anyway, whipping her head around and gasping. Jake seemed taller, his shoulders seemed even wider, his face harder. His hand had clamped down on her flesh like a vise and she knew there was no way she could get away from him.

CHAPTER THREE

"HI SARA," JAKE said, looking down at the bundle she carried.

She glared at him and clutched her baby up against her chest.

"So this is my little girl, is it?" he asked softly.

She quickly suppressed her original reaction. There was, after all, no place to run to while they were on the ferry.

"Hello, Jake," she said. She couldn't pretend to be pleased to see him, but she didn't think screaming would do her any good. "Fancy meeting you in a place like this."

He raised an eyebrow. "I'm sure you expected to see me again," he said, his voice low and not particularly friendly. "You didn't think you were going to get away that easily, did you?"

She gave him a look of round-eyed innocence. "Get away from what, pray tell?"

"You know exactly what I'm talking about. I'm sure you've talked to the agency by now." He shook his head, bemused. "I knew you were a runner from the start."

"A runner?" She held her temper with a lot of effort. "Why would I run from you, Jake? Is there something I should know?" Her gaze narrowed. "In what way are you trying to threaten me?"

His mouth twisted. "I'm sure you've figured it out by now. I'm that little girl's biological father."

She knew he thought that, but still, hearing him say the words made her cringe. For just a few seconds, she was breathless, but she pulled herself together quickly.

"No kidding? Where's your proof?"

He released her arm as though he'd decided she wasn't going to run just yet. "All in good time," he said softly.

She shook her head. If he thought he was going to bully her, he could think again. "Not good enough, Jake. You see, I've had this baby with me for six months now. I've mothered her. I've cared for her. I've loved her. I've done all the paperwork, paid all the fees. I've been inspected, injected and detected, as the old song might say. I've been found to be qualified." Her eyes flashed. "What have you been found to be?"

He blinked at her and she could tell she'd actually made him think for just a moment.

"It's coming," he said at last, sounding a bit more defensive. "It'll be proven soon."

That gave her a small surge of hope.

"In other words, you've got nothing. Meanwhile, I've got all the official seals of approval I could possibly get. This baby and I have bonded, big time." She had to stop to keep her voice from breaking. Taking a deep breath, she went on. "In order to even think about breaking that bond, you're going to have to come up with some heavy-duty evidence. I'm not giving up easy."

She glared at him. He glared right back. She could almost see sparks flying between them. This was no good and she knew it. But she couldn't stop. She had to let him know how much this meant to her. He couldn't be allowed to treat this as a lark of some kind. He had to know the consequences were serious.

He shrugged. "I may not have signed as many official forms as you have, but I've been tested. The DNA results will trump all your seals and certificates and…" He paused for a moment as though he regretted having to say it. "And all your emotional appeal, Sara. I'm sorry, but that's reality."

She knew he was right and it made her want to sob, but she couldn't let him see weakness. "We'll see about that," she said.

Funny, but she'd been so scared when she was running from him. Now that he'd caught her, the fear was gone. There was a dark, burning anger deep inside her, and a determination that was growing stronger every minute. She knew only one thing for sure—she would not give up her baby. She would find a way.

He gestured in her direction and she flinched. It was an obvious move. His gaze met hers.

"Why would I hurt you?" he asked her, seemingly irritated by her reaction.

"I didn't think you were going to hurt me,"

she said coolly. "I just don't want you to touch her."

A series of emotions crossed his face but she wasn't sure what it all meant. The only thought that came to her was, *So this is what it's like to have an enemy. Scary.*

He looked out toward Seattle and seemed to settle his anger down. When he turned back toward her, his eyes were cold but his face was smooth. No emotions showing at all.

"Could I hold her?" he asked quietly.

She pressed Savannah closer, holding her tightly. This was painful. She just couldn't do it. "She's sleeping," she said.

"No, she's not. I can see her eyes. They're wide-open. Just let me hold her for a minute."

"No," she said, feeling fierce. "Not here. Not yet."

He stared down at her, not saying a word, but warning her that he could do whatever he wanted to do if he felt like it. At least, that was the message she took from the look in his eyes.

"There's a security guard on this ferry," she said quickly. "I could yell for help."

His wide mouth twisted in half a grin. "You could. But you won't."

She looked away and rocked Savannah softly. "What makes you think you know so much about how I tick?"

"I'm a student of everyday psychology. I knew from the way you ran at the café that you would try to get away with your..." He stopped, realizing that was the wrong thing for him to admit. "With the baby. You knew from the first that I have an unshakable claim."

"I don't know anything of the sort." She shifted Savannah to her other shoulder. "We have a long way to go before we can tell for sure just who you are."

He turned away and looked out over the rushing water as though working hard on controlling his temper. It took him some time to get to the point where he could turn back and she wondered if he was counting to a lot more than ten. When he finally turned back, his face was calm but his eyes were flashing.

"When the DNA results arrive in my favor—which they will—you'll have to give way. How long did you say you've had her?"

"Six months."

"Six months." He shrugged. "Yeah, that's a good long time. But facts are facts. She's my baby and it's my responsibility to take care of her."

Sara pressed her lips together. She had plenty she could say but she wasn't going to muddy the waters right now. There would be time to make her case. Right now he had her in a corner. It looked like everything was going his way. But she was beginning to realize that she had many cards of her own that she could play. This thing wasn't a done deal yet.

"Look, Sara," he said impatiently. "I know you've checked this out with the agency. You know who I am. Let me hold her."

She shook her head.

He raked fingers through his thick, auburn hair. His frustration was clear, but she held her ground, realizing that she'd better put it into words so he could deal with it.

"Jake, you're a stranger right now. I don't know if you're who you say you are. We're standing on a boat, right over the ocean. Anything could happen. I can't risk it."

He frowned and actually looked hurt. "I wouldn't do anything that could possibly harm her."

Sara held her ground. "I'm not letting you hold her."

For just a moment, anger flared in his eyes. She saw it and the sense of its intensity stopped her heart for a beat. He was scary in a way she'd never known with a man before.

"All right," he said at last, his voice raw. "I guess I can understand that." A muscle worked at his jawline, but he smiled. "I can even commend you for taking good care of my baby." He took a deep breath. "But we need to talk somewhere. Somewhere safe."

She didn't want to talk to him. What was the point? She knew what he wanted. He knew what she demanded. Neither one of them was going to budge an inch.

Mentally she shook herself. She was going to have to talk to him. That was the only way she could get him to see how crazy this was. There were so many angles to fight this from. Right now, she thought she had the strongest—he wasn't father material.

It was true. He didn't know the first thing

about babies. She remembered how he'd been with a kitchen and she almost smiled. He wasn't domesticated in any way at all. He was hopeless. He had to learn that somehow. And who else was going to make him face it if she didn't?

"All right." She sighed, letting him hear her exasperation. "Come back to my sister's house with me. My brother-in-law should be home by now. I'd be more comfortable if he and my sister were there, too."

"Okay. You've got a deal." He seemed relieved, glancing at the rapidly approaching coastline and noting that they were almost at the end of this part of their ferry journey.

She hated that he went to the car with them for the ride back, but she knew it would be petty to insist he stay out on the deck. They got into the car and he looked around, his mouth twisted.

"What the hell did you think you were doing?" he asked her.

She lifted her chin and shrugged. "I'm taking my baby for a drive. I don't think there are any laws against that."

"That's not your baby," he growled. "That's my baby."

She blinked quickly and kept her composure. "We don't know that yet, do we?"

"I know it."

They didn't speak again for a long time. She drove the car off the ferry and then back on again. Savannah played with her fingers, made some noises that sounded like she was trying to sing, then dozed off. Jake sat twisted in his seat, watching her every minute.

Sara turned on the radio and soft music played, hiding the awkwardness of the silence. When they were about halfway back across the bay, she couldn't resist asking him a few questions.

"So how did you get on the ferry without me seeing you?"

He shrugged. "I was already on board. I've been waiting since you left the café."

"I see."

"Right after you left, I asked around the place to see if anyone knew who you were. The girl working behind the counter said she thought your name was Sara." He shrugged. "So then I knew."

She nodded. "Of course," she said softly, staring intently at the car in front of them.

"But I knew you weren't living in the house next to me, as you were supposed to be. I didn't know where to find you. So I hung around the ferry and waited for you to make a run for it." He turned and narrowed his eyes, looking at her. "Did you know who I was from the start? Why didn't you tell me you had a little girl?"

She shook her head. "No, I didn't know. And until I realized who you were, I was just waiting for a chance to tell you about her. You were pretty much monopolizing the conversation, you know. I could hardly get a word in."

He looked surprised. "Funny. I usually think of myself as the strong, silent type."

She rolled her eyes. "Right."

He looked back at the baby, now asleep in the car seat. "She's gorgeous," he said, his mouth turning up at the corners. "You kind of fall in love with her at first sight, don't you?"

Sara felt tears stinging her eyes but she would die before she let him know his words had affected her. She stared at him for a long moment, wishing she could see into his heart.

"I have to be very careful around you," she said softly at last. "You're a seducer."

"What?" He was outraged. "I haven't touched you!"

She shook her head. "I don't mean that way. I mean that you're a seducer of the mind. If I'm not careful, I'll end up letting you convince me to do something I shouldn't."

"Oh." He relaxed, and then his mouth twisted in something resembling humor. "Well, I can't help that."

"Yes, you can. You're the exact reason it's going to happen."

He frowned at her, not sure what she was getting at. "Look, mind games are not my thing."

"Really?" This was good. He was unsure. Without that massive swagger and confidence, he seemed almost manageable. "What is your thing, Jake? What is important to you?"

"Right now? That baby." He jerked his head in her direction.

Sara's lips tightened. "Her name is Savannah."

"Really?" He frowned thoughtfully. "I was

thinking about naming her Jolene. My mother's name was Jolene. Or so they tell me."

"Jolene," Sara said with scorn, glancing at him. "She isn't a Jolene at all. Just look at her."

"Oh, yeah? What's a Jolene look like?"

She threw up a hand. "Different from this."

He frowned, studying Savannah's face as though he was going to find the right name for her if he stared hard enough. But instead, he went off in another direction.

"So why are you staying at your sister's house?" he asked.

"My house is being renovated."

He nodded. "I've seen the workmen come and go. It looks like you're adding on a whole wing."

"I am." She glanced at him sideways. "It's for Savannah. A bedroom, a bathroom and a playroom. All for her." She bit her lip and then continued, her voice shaking. "You see, we have a life planned out. How can you just swoop in and smash it to bits?"

He shook his head, looking almost regretful. "I didn't set this all up on purpose, Sara. There's nothing personal in it. It's just the way the cards fell. No one's fault."

No one's fault. Then whom did she go to in order to make her case?

They landed and the cars drove off, one after another. She turned hers toward Jill's street. Her house was high up on the hill, visible from everywhere on this side of the island. She got to the corner of the turn up to her sister's house and suddenly Jake held his hand out.

"Hold it," he said. "Pull over."

"What is it?" She did as he ordered, but looked around suspiciously. There was a large, tough-looking man standing on the corner. His nose appeared as if it had been broken a couple of times. His hair was clipped close to his head and he was dressed in worn black leather and torn jeans. He could have been a stand-in for a member of The Dirty Dozen. Just looking at him made her shiver.

She glanced at Jake. He and the man had made eye contact. Neither one of them gave any indication of greeting or of even knowing each other, but there was something about their body language that made it clear they were acquaintances. The stare was enough.

"Okay, I'm going to have to take a rain check on that meeting," Jake said.

She gaped at him. "What?"

How could he dismiss it like this? To her, getting some sort of resolution and doing it as soon as possible was as necessary as breathing. Her whole life hung in the balance, and he was ready to walk off and do it later? And all because of some guy standing on a corner?

"Who is that man?" she demanded.

"Someone I have to talk to," he said, unbuckling his seat belt. "I can't explain. Not now. I'll have to catch you later." He pulled out his cell phone. "Give me your phone number. I'll call you."

She recited it automatically, frowning and wondering what to make of this strange man. He punched in the numbers, leaned over the back of the seat and looked at Savannah, sighing.

"I need to get to know this little one," he muttered as he straightened and turned away. "That house there at the top? That's where you're staying?"

"Yes."

He hesitated, looking at her probingly. "You're not going to run again, are you?"

"I wasn't running before."

"Yes, you were."

She looked toward where the sea made a silver line on the horizon.

He grunted and looked there, too. "I'm going to have to trust you," he said. "But I think you know better than to go off again. I'll go to the end of the earth to find you, if you do. And the reunion won't be pretty."

She snapped her head back around to face him. "Oh, stop with the threats. Please! We're both grown-ups. We can talk things over without the TV show theatrics. This is real life, not some silly drama."

A reluctant smile broke out on his hard face. "You see, that's just the thing about you, Sara. I liked you from the beginning." His eyebrows rose. "I hope I'm not going to have to change my mind about that."

Her eyes flashed. "You know what? It doesn't matter if you do. We have an issue between us, something that has to be resolved. But whether we like each other is irrelevant. Who cares?"

"Right." He nodded firmly. "Who cares." He glanced at the man on the corner and looked back at her. "Okay. See you in the morning."

She watched him walk away. The man who had been waiting turned and walked with him. The two of them looked like something out of a 1930s gangster movie.

"What in the world?" she said aloud, shaking her head as she watched them go. This whole situation was getting stranger and stranger. Maybe it was going to be a silly drama after all. Who knew?

But the one thing she was sure of—she wasn't letting her baby go off with a man like this. Impossible to imagine. It would never happen. She would find a way.

CHAPTER FOUR

SARA FELT AS though every nerve in her system was quivering with energy. There was so much to think about, so many plans to make—so many traps to set. First of all she had to find out more about this man, this Jake Martin—and how he'd met her half sister Kelly, Savannah's mother.

Was he a good guy? Mixed evidence so far. Were things going to pop up that would be relevant and interesting to the agency as to his fitness to be a father?

Oh, come on. There had to be something.

In the morning, he would arrive and they would sit down in Jill's breakfast room, sipping coffee and eating one of her sister's wonderful Bundt cakes. And they would talk.

She turned the car up the driveway to Jill's, planning the assault on Jake's character as though it was the D-day invasion. This was a fight she had to win. The thought of giving her baby over to this stranger made her sick with revulsion. It couldn't happen. If she had only a few hours before she was going to see him again, she was going to spend that time preparing for battle.

Sara looked up from feeding her baby from a bottle and forced a smile as Jill came into the kitchen, clutching her long white robe around her.

"Morning," she said with brittle cheer.

Jill seemed incredulous. "What on earth are you doing up so early?" She paused to kiss the top of Savannah's head, then went on to the coffeemaker. "I've got twelve cakes to bake for the Alliance Ladies or I would still be happily sleeping away myself."

"Sleep?" Sara said groggily. "What is this thing you call sleep?"

Jill groaned. "You haven't slept a wink, have you?"

Sara shrugged. "I think I did get a few minutes worth around 3:00 a.m. My mind was whirring like a windup toy and I couldn't stop.

I had to think, to go over all the possibilities. So I came down here where I could begin making lists." She nodded toward the three or four pages of wild note taking that were scattered across the table.

Jill poured herself a cup of coffee and came back to sink into the seat opposite her sister.

"Listen. We'll do it all. No stone left unturned. We'll research and brainstorm and write letters. We'll start calling people today and…"

Sara smiled lovingly at Jill and shook her head. "I've already been doing all those things. It's three hours earlier on the East Coast. I've called three different sources back there already."

Jill gaped at her sister, impressed. Sara had always been the careful one, her hair stylishly sleek, her makeup perfect, her goals clear and well-supported by her actions. Meanwhile, Jill seemed to be all over the place, just like her unruly mop of curly blond hair. And yet, Jill was the older sister and they both knew she would be there for Sara no matter what.

"Who did you talk to? What did you find out?"

"First I called the agency again to see if I couldn't get more information. I wanted to know about forms I could fill out and channels I could go through to file an appeal, just in case. They were adamant. There is supposedly nothing I can do."

"Nothing?"

"So I was told. If the DNA comes in his favor and he is deemed to be her father, that's it. Game over."

She stared at Jill with tears shimmering in her eyes. "I mean—that's it. He takes her. We wave goodbye and it's over. He walks off with her." Her face was tragic. "How can this be? It's just not right."

Jill nodded slowly. "I know, darling. It doesn't feel right at all. It feels unfair and dangerous. Maybe if we talk to the people at the agency…"

"That's exactly who I've been talking to. And I did leave a message for Mrs. Truesdale to call me back. She's the one who's always been the most helpful."

Jill closed her eyes, trying to think. "Who else can we call? Who else did you contact?"

"I called Mark Trainor. He's a lawyer at the

magazine. I worked with him on a few features in the past. I've known him for years and I knew he'd give me the straight scoop."

Jill looked hopeful. "Well?"

Sara sighed. "He told me he'd be glad to recommend someone who deals with adoptions. He knows someone who would be especially good with the paperwork and going for appeals, or whatever." She shook her head sadly. "But he didn't advise going that way."

"Why not?"

"He didn't think there was much use fighting it. He thought I'd probably end up spending a lot of money and going through a lot of heartbreak with nothing to show for it in the end."

She looked down at the baby in her arms. Savannah had stopped drinking and let the bottle slip away. Her gaze was fixed completely on Sara's face. Suddenly she smiled and her pure, innocent love seemed to fill the room.

"Oh, sweetest heart, I just can't, can't…!" She stopped the words before they left her lips. She couldn't let her baby know in any way what loomed before them. Tears filled her eyes and began to make trails down her face.

Savannah's laugh sounded like a series of hiccups. She laughed as though Sara was the funniest thing she'd seen in ages. She laughed despite Sara's tears, and Sara began to smile because of her.

Jill watched, tears in her own eyes.

"Tell you what," she said. "Let's have a piece of cake. I've got something to tell you about."

Sara looked up at her and grinned through her tears. "Oh, you and your Bundt cake. You think it's like chicken soup, the cure for everything. Staying here with you, I'm getting fat."

Jill got down the cake anyway and began to cut slices with a long, beautifully carved cake knife.

"See, that's what I've always envied about you," she told her sister as she worked. "You never get fat. You're about as thin as those models your magazine plasters all over every page, wearing the latest outfits to come down the pike." She put a piece of Lemon Delight on a small plate and handed it to Sara. "Meanwhile, I'm pudging up. And it's going to be about nine months before I can really go on a diet again."

Sara stared at her. "Wait a minute. Do you mean...?"

Jill's face broke out in a joyful smile. "Yes. Connor and I are going to have a baby."

Sara gasped and looked stricken. "Already?" Jill and her husband had only been married for three months. Somehow Sara was starting to feel that everything was moving too fast, everything was spinning out of control.

All the joy drained from Jill's face and she frowned resentfully. She'd obviously expected a better response.

"I didn't know I had a schedule to keep," she snapped.

"No, I mean..." Sara shook her head, knowing she was handling this badly, but she was genuinely worried. She'd been here all along. She'd seen the chaos Jill's life had been only months before.

In fact, when the news about Kelly's death and Savannah's existence first came to light, there had been a discussion as to which sister could manage to take on this new little life, and Jill, though she'd been willing, had made it clear it would truly be a hardship for her. And now, only a short time later, she was ready to take on a new baby again. "Well, you can barely handle the twins as it is. Do you really think…?"

Jill glared at her. "No, Sara, you've got it wrong. That was the old me. That was the unmarried me." She read the concern on Sara's face and her attitude softened. Reaching out, she took her sister's hands. "Oh, Sara, look at me. Things are completely different. I've got a wonderful husband now. We can do this. Together." She smiled, coaxing out the Sara that she'd hoped to find there.

"Oh. Of course." Sara relaxed. She knew she was too careful sometimes. She really had to loosen up a little. "I guess that does make a difference."

"It makes all the difference in the world," Jill said.

"Okay then." Sara lifted her baby and rose, swinging her around the room in a happiness dance. "Savannah, you've got a new cousin coming." She looked at Jill. "Boy or girl?"

Jill shrugged. "We're going to wait until the

six months mark and then we'll decide if we want to know ahead of time."

"Ah, you always were a sucker for tradition."

Jill rose and opened her arms and they had a group hug.

"I really am happy for you, sweetie," Sara said, giving her a squeeze. "It's just that I worry…"

"I know. So do I. But we're family and we'll make sure it all comes out okay. Won't we?"

"Of course."

They sat down again to finish their cake and talk over the preparations for the baby.

"How is Connor taking it?" Sara asked.

Jill laughed. "He's so funny. On the one hand, he's excited. On the other, he's scared."

Sara nodded. "Just the way I was when Savannah came into my life." She seemed stricken as she remembered the threat that was looming over her. "And now, the fear is so much greater," she said softly.

Jill reached out and covered her hand. "When do you think he'll show up?"

They both knew whom she was talking about.

Sara shrugged. "I know so little about him, it's hard to tell. He could show up for morning coffee, or he could wait until he gets some business cleared up in the morning. Don't forget, he's not supposed to be here at all. Not legally."

"Okay, so we'll just go on with our normal lives, drinking coffee and baking, etc, as though this hadn't happened."

"How can we possibly do that?"

"We can try. You want to keep Savannah happy and smiling, don't you?"

"Of course. Whatever else happens, that's the most important thing."

"Actually the most important thing is keeping Savannah safe."

Jill picked up their plates and started toward the sink with them. She stopped short just before she reached it, staring out the tall kitchen windows toward the play area of her backyard.

"Sara," she said sharply. "What does he look like?"

Sara made a face. "Tall and big and scary."

"Thick auburn hair?"

Sara looked up, alarmed. "Yes."

"I think that's him, then."

"What?" Sara slid out of the seat and moved quickly to stand beside her sister. "Oh, my gosh!"

There he was sitting in one of the larger swings hanging on the swing set, rocking a bit, back and forth.

She gripped Jill's shoulder. "Call the police."

"Sara! No. He's just waiting for you out there. He's not doing anything threatening."

"Just his existence is threatening." She folded her arms in tightly, trying to keep control of the fear she felt. "He has no right to stalk us."

Jill turned and searched her sister's eyes, taking her hands and looking worried. "Sara, darling, calm down. We have to be reasonable. He hasn't done anything wrong."

"Not yet, maybe. Just wait."

Jill sighed. "Listen, sweetie, he may be Savannah's father, and if he is, that means he was close to Kelly. Kelly's our half sister, and even though we were never very close to her, she was a part of our family. That makes his attachment to our family clear, doesn't it? You can't treat him like a total stranger. We owe it to him to at least be polite."

"Polite!"

"Yes."

Sara groaned. "I wish…I wish…"

"We all wish. But we have to take what we get and learn to deal with it." She hugged her sister. "Come on. Go on out there and invite him in."

Sara looked at her, horrified. "I will not. He'll want to hold Savannah."

"Of course. And we'll be here. He won't hurt her."

Sara was shaking her head. "I don't think I have to let him hold her. Not until he has proof."

Jill pulled back and shrugged. "It's up to you. But just remember, the harder you make it for him, the harder he'll probably make it for you if things change. Be prepared."

A shiver of nausea swept through Sara at her sister's words. She wouldn't even let her mind go there. She was not going to have to give up her baby. Somehow, someway…

Taking a deep breath, she turned toward the sliding glass door. "Will you watch her?" she threw back over her shoulder. Savannah was beginning to make "hey, don't forget about me!" sounds from her chair at the table.

"Sure," Jill said quickly. "Listen, I'll take her up to help me get the boys out of bed. If you decide to bring him in, we won't even be here in the kitchen until you signal you're ready."

Sara nodded and started out. This had to be done, but she was dreading it. Maybe she could get him to leave.

Jake had watched the sun come up over the mountains. He'd paced the waterfront and then turned up toward Jill's house. After waiting outside for what seemed like hours and finding no sign of life inside, he'd found his way into the backyard, hoping he'd get noticed and invited in. He didn't want to have to get tough about this. A nice friendly invitation would be better than an angry demand. But his patience was only human. The invite had better come pretty soon.

The yard was large and included a sloping lawn and a sand play area with a swing set. That seemed to mean there were other children here.

Children. What the hell did he know about children? Even less than he knew about kitchens. But he was going to have to learn. The question was—could he?

He hadn't put it that starkly to himself before. He'd been ignoring reality and living on dreams. He'd been riding along in the wash of the wave that had crashed over him the day he realized he had a child of his own. What had happened in his kitchen the day before had forced him to begin to face some home truths. He wasn't equipped to take care of a baby. He was going to have to get up to speed fast. Another life depended on it.

He had a baby. Wow. He looked up at the windows of Jill's house, wondering which ones led to the room where his baby slept. He'd been home from his time in South East Asia for almost two weeks before he read the letter that told him about Savannah. He knew he had a stack of mail from Kelly, but he'd avoided reading it. They'd met when he was on R and R in Hawaii. They had a lovely time for almost two weeks. But they'd both said from the first that they wanted to keep things light and fun—nothing serious. Now here were all these letters from her. It looked like she'd changed her mind—but he hadn't.

Finally he steeled himself and opened up the first one. Just what he'd been afraid of—she was pregnant. He'd groaned. He was so careful to make sure things like that didn't happen. He knew what it was like to grow up without proper parenting and he would never want to inflict that on a child.

He opened the other letters and skimmed them quickly, noting her anger at first when he didn't respond, then her horror when she found out he was missing in action and presumed captured by the enemy. There was only one letter after Savannah was born, but it gave all the details. Kelly seemed to have accepted that he was probably dead and was just straightening out the loose ends of what had been their relationship.

He'd stayed up for hours, brooding about what to do. He tried to remember what she looked like. She'd been pretty with huge green eyes and lots of flaming red curls. As he remembered it, she'd been a vivacious sort, always ready to try anything from surfing to mountain climbing. She'd had a quick tendency to laugh—and a tendency to tease. He'd found her half adorable and half annoying.

They'd had a lot of fun together. But he hadn't loved her, and she hadn't seemed to care at the time.

Later, she obviously did. But there hadn't been any letters for over six months. He agonized over how to contact her. He even tried to talk himself out of doing it at all. Maybe she was married now. Maybe she wouldn't want him interfering in her life after all this time. But he always came back to the bottom line— he had a baby. A little girl. Someone that was truly tied to him in ways he'd never experienced before. He couldn't let go of that fact.

First thing in the morning, he tried to contact her. Her return address was in Virginia, not far from where he was in Washington, D.C. When he couldn't get a phone number, he went by the apartment and talked to the manager. And that was how he found out that Kelly had died in a car accident months before.

The tragedy of her passing hit him hard, but anxiety about the baby came even stronger. He started right away, haunting every Federal office he could think of that might have a bearing on this situation, and finally, he found the Children's Agency and found out that Savannah had been sent to live with her aunt in Washington State.

He began the process of proving his claim right away, but he couldn't stand the wait. Patience was not his main virtue, and he headed for the Pacific Coast as soon as he'd finished doing all he could at the agency. He quickly rented a house right next door to where Savannah was supposedly living, only to find it empty. And then, Sara had come knocking on his door.

He hadn't realized who she was at first, but now he knew. She had his baby. And he was going to have to force himself to wait. But not for long. Because Savannah was his.

He heard the slider and looked up to see Sara coming toward him. She wasn't carrying the baby, and that was all he cared about. But he had to admit the morning sun turned her hair into spun gold and she looked trim and determined walking toward him. She had something that belonged to him and he meant to end up with it, but all in all, she wasn't a bad sort. He'd actually liked her before he found out who she was.

She stopped a few feet away and stared at him. "Have you cleaned up your kitchen yet?" she asked.

"What?" He frowned at her, rapidly beginning to revamp his opinion of her. What a completely off-the-wall thing to ask. "No. Who has time to worry about kitchens?"

Now she was frowning, too. "You do. The Lancasters are nice people and you've ruined their kitchen. You're going to have to fix it."

He waved that away. "All in good time."

She didn't like the sound of that. If he was going to be a father, he'd better learn some responsibility. "I'll call someone to come over and give you an estimate," she said crisply.

He stared at her and half laughed. She was like a dog with a bone.

"Listen, I don't want to talk about kitchens. I want to talk about Savannah."

"Okay." She knew that, of course. She slid into the swing hanging next to his. "Talk."

He hesitated. What could he say that he hadn't already said?

She took advantage of the pause. "Here's the deal." She gazed at him levelly, her dark eyes snapping with intensity. "Savannah is officially mine. I've got the paperwork to prove it. There's nothing really to discuss about that." She waved an arm dramatically. "You appear out of nowhere and claim certain things. Who knows if you're telling the truth or not? I'm not going to move on your say-so. Once you have some paperwork to prove your case, we'll talk."

She settled back and began to move the swing as though that settled everything.

He shook his head. She was trying to fend him off, make him slink into the shadows and wait his turn. But she had a surprise coming if she thought he would go so easily. It wasn't his style.

"Not good enough," he told her stonily. "That could take another week or more."

She glanced at him sideways. "Look, be reasonable. We have no way of knowing anything about you. You can't expect us to welcome you with open arms. You're a complete stranger."

He shrugged. "So what do you want to know about me? Ask me anything."

She stopped the swing and turned to face him. "Okay. Why not? Let's start with this."

She drew in a deep breath. "Who was that man last night? And why was talking to him more important than Savannah?"

For just a moment, there was an evasive look in his eyes. "That had nothing to do with Savannah," he said quickly. "It...he's a buddy of mine. We were in the Rangers together. He came to ask for my help." He turned his face toward the distant ocean. "We've got the sort of relationship—well, when he needs me, I'm there for him." He turned back to meet her gaze, his own open and candid. "You can know that about me. Loyalty to the men I served with. That's number one. End of story."

She stared at him, then transferred her gaze to the ground. "So you're saying that your buddies from the service come first with you. Your priorities start right there with them."

"No, that's not what I'm saying." But he hesitated, wondering if that was true. "Your own child is in a whole different category. All that other stuff has nothing to do with her."

She nodded, listening. "I think it has a lot to do with Savannah," she said softly. "It has to do with you and what your motivations are.

What drives you. What's really important in your life."

He shook his head, almost bemused. "Now you're reaching, Sara," he said. "Let it go."

Let it go? Hah!

"Tell me this," she said coolly. "Have you ever had a baby before?"

His head went back. "No, of course not."

She leaned toward him like a prosecutor. "Have you ever taken care of one?"

"No."

She leaned even closer, as though she was about to get in his face. "Have you ever lived with one?"

"Have you?" he shot back. "What did you know about babies? Before Savannah, I mean."

She pulled back but there was a triumphant smile just barely curling the corners of her mouth. "My sister Jill has twins. I helped her with them from the beginning." She sighed. "I had a pretty good idea of what I was getting into. And I don't think you have a clue."

He stared at her. Was she serious? "So that's the tact you're going to take, is it? I'm incompetent? I'm too clueless to know how to take care of a baby? I won't know what I'm doing, and therefore shouldn't be allowed to have her? Is that going to be the basis for your appeal?"

She stiffened. "Who says I'm filing an appeal?"

"Of course you will. You'll mount one as soon as I take charge of Savannah. I know damn well you've already called a lawyer."

She flushed.

He nodded. "Bingo," he said softly.

"Of course I've talked to a lawyer," she said. "And you should, too. We've got to make sure all the i's are dotted and the t's are crossed."

"Thanks for the warning." He looked up and stiffened. "Uh-oh. Looks like you're getting reinforcements."

CHAPTER FIVE

Sara looked up and saw Jill's handsome husband, Connor, walking toward them. His look was wary but not unfriendly.

"Jake Martin?" he said, holding out his hand. "I'm Sara's brother-in-law, Connor McNair."

Jake rose from the swing and extended his own hand. "It's a pleasure," he said.

"Jill would like to meet you," Connor said, looking at Sara but ignoring her ferocious glare. "Why don't you come on in and have some coffee? Jill's a baker and she's saved you a special slice of her latest Bundt cake." Connor smiled and turned his collar up against the stiff breeze. "It will be a more comfortable place to talk."

"Sounds good."

Sara pushed back the sense of outrage

building in her chest. It sure seemed like she was outnumbered. Hopefully Connor had a plan. Otherwise, whose side was he on?

But she kept her confusion to herself. Jake was going to get his chance to hold Savannah. She knew it had to happen sometime. Might as well get it over with.

They walked up a brick path to the house and went in. Sara watched Jake as he met Jill, suddenly reminded of how good-looking he was. He was turning on the charm, but surely they could see through that.

"If you don't mind, I'd really like to see my…Savannah," he said, looking around the kitchen as though he thought she might be somewhere close.

"She's in the other room. I'll go get her."

"No," Sara said, so softly she wasn't sure if the others had heard her.

But Jill turned and took her hands. "Sara, I think it's only right. We're all here. Nothing will happen."

She knew her sister was right but it was killing her. She closed her eyes for a few seconds, then tried to smile. "Let me get her, then."

"All right."

Savannah was lying on her tummy in her play crib, playing with a touch toy. She looked up with a beatific smile when Sara came into view, her huge blue eyes set off by her golden curls. "Mama!" she cried, pounding her fist into the plastic toy. "Mama, Mama, Mama."

Sara's eyes filled with tears but she blinked them back. She wasn't going to let herself fall apart every time she looked at her baby.

"Come here, sweet thing," she said as she pulled her up and carried her to the changing table. She wanted to dress her in something pretty. There was no point in doing anything else. She was a pretty baby and no amount of downplaying that was going to work in dissuading Jake from taking her. He was going to love her no matter what. How could he help it?

As she carried Savannah into the kitchen where Jill was plying Jake with Bundt cake, she couldn't help but feel a glow of pride.

"Here she is," she said, announcing her and holding her up for inspection, right in front of the large, rough person who claimed to be her father. "This is a man named Jake Martin," she whispered in her ear. "Can you smile at him please? Can you say 'hi'?"

Savannah stuck her fist in her mouth and stared at him for a long moment. He stared back, looking thunderstruck, as though he'd never seen anything like her before. At last, she smiled. He smiled back, and it was like ice breaking in the Arctic. Something passed between the two of them, some flash of recognition or acknowledgment, the establishment of a special bond—Sara didn't know exactly what it was but she felt a pain in her heart such as she'd never felt before.

Was it really so obvious...so simple? Did blood connect across the air between them? Would she just be left behind?

He didn't ask to hold Savannah. Sara expected it, had been tense, not sure how she would react. Waiting, she couldn't breathe, but he didn't ask.

Then a thought flashed into her head like a bolt from the blue. He hadn't asked to hold Savannah—because now that he'd evaluated the situation, he was scared to. He didn't know how to hold her. He didn't know what to do and in front of her whole family, he wasn't going to risk it.

Interesting. And somehow invigorating. Maybe all wasn't lost, after all. Maybe she still had a chance in this sweepstakes.

He'd come to take her baby away, but he just wasn't ready. From what she'd seen, he'd done nothing in his life that could prepare him for it. And even if he got beyond that, he would soon find out he didn't like what child raising entailed. At least, she would bet that would be the way he would go.

That was the angle she had to take. She had to learn how to cajole him and convince him that this was not what he wanted to do. Much better to use sympathy and examples rather than confrontation and anger. There might be a possibility of success that way. It would be tough to hold back her temper, but she could do it if she thought it could get her anywhere.

They sat in the kitchen and ate cake and watched Savannah play with her toys in the middle of the floor. Connor and Jill seemed to have a thousand things to discuss with Jake. Sara didn't listen to most of it. She was thinking, plotting, hoping.

At the same time, she did notice how friendly the three of them seemed to be getting. That gave her a weird feeling, almost like jealousy. Surely her own family wasn't going to end up being on Jake's side in this. Were they?

No, impossible. They loved Savannah almost as much as she did. There was no way they would help him take her away from the place where she belonged. But Jill was concerned about keeping a happy face on things.

"Why don't you and Jake take Savannah to the park?" she suggested. She gave Sara a significant look, as if hinting they should get to know each other better.

"Oh." Sara wasn't sure how much she wanted to be alone with him.

The funny thing was, Jake appeared a little hesitant about it himself.

"Great idea," he said gamely. Then his blue eyes brightened. "Why not take the boys, too?"

Sara stared at him. Did he have any idea what he was suggesting? No, he didn't. And that was why she smiled and said, "Yes. Let's take the twins. They love the park."

She knew they would be a handful. There was more energy stored in the two of them than the average windmill could generate in a year. They could take apart a house in fifteen minutes and leave their keeper with days and days of rehab. Just a few months before, they'd locked their babysitter outside and ransacked the upstairs, throwing things out of windows. She was pretty sure she could depend on them to create some sort of chaos.

The walk to the park was nice. She put Savannah in a stroller and they let the twins run free. The street they took only rarely saw a car and the boys stayed close enough so that it wasn't a worry. There were plenty of neighbors working in their yards. She waved to the ones she knew.

The boys were wearing their Danny Duck capes that Jill had made them, held on by Velcro tabs. *Danny Duck* was their favorite TV show. They called him "Dandan Duck," but it worked for them. As they ran, their little capes spread out behind them, and they laughed and pretended to fly.

"Dandan Duck!" they called back and forth. The end of summer was coming. She could feel it in the breeze. There was always a tinge of sadness at losing those lazy, hazy days, but it also meant the holidays weren't far away. She looked down at Savannah, laughing in her stroller as she spotted a cat across the street. Would she be able to spend her baby's first Christmas with her? Or would it all be over by then?

Jake had been silent so far, but now he spoke. "This is nice," he said, then made a face as though he regretted being so uninspiring. "I mean, it's great to get a chance to go to the park with kids. I've never done it before."

Good, Sara thought to herself. *This can be a learning experience for you.*

Out loud, she noted, "Children love going to the park. The problem is usually getting them to leave when time is up."

He shrugged, looking cocky. "Hey, they don't call me The Enforcer for nothing."

She frowned. She really didn't like the sound of that.

He saw her frown and winced, knowing he'd said something he shouldn't have again. But what else was new? He did it all the time. Usually it didn't matter. He expected people to take him as he was, or get lost. That was the way he'd always lived.

He gazed down at the little girl in the stroller and his heart swelled with some sort of emotion he couldn't even put a name to. His little girl. A lump rose in his throat as he thought of it. He'd have to make some changes. He had to throw out that old, rough way of living and learn to do things right. She deserved as much. He had to make himself worthy of her.

And how was he going to learn to do all these things? Who was going to teach him? There weren't a lot of women with child rearing experience in his life. Right now Sara was the prime candidate. He needed what she could do to help him. She was just about his only hope. The problem was, she didn't like him much.

He couldn't blame her. He was her worst nightmare. But he couldn't get bogged down in that. His goal was to make himself into the best dad Savannah could hope for. And he was beginning to realize, that was going to take a lot of work.

He glanced at Sara again. What did you do

when you wanted to make a woman like you? He'd never dealt with this before. If a woman didn't like him, he shrugged and turned to a woman who did. There were always plenty of those. So what was his strategy to gain Sara's favor?

It made him grin to think of it. Good thing she couldn't read his mind. He moved closer so he could talk without others overhearing.

"Sara, I'm sorry about this. I didn't plan it this way. I didn't even know Savannah existed until last week." He shrugged and tried to look engagingly charming. "Things happen."

She nodded but she didn't plan to tumble to his charm offensive. "Yes, things happen. I understand that." She took a deep breath and plunged in. "And you want to be a father to this baby. I don't blame you. Who wouldn't want to be?" She gestured toward her, the proof if any was needed. "She's adorable and wonderful—everything you could ever want in a child."

She folded her arms and lifted her chin. "But the results of the DNA tests haven't come in yet." She eyed him warningly. He had to understand this was only the beginning.

"What I think we need to do is take some time to get to know each other. Talk things over. See how it looks to you after some time here."

She gave him about half a smile. That was all she could muster. "We'll see how things work out."

He took what she had to say in good cheer, to her surprise. The confrontational man from the ferry seemed to have vanished from sight.

"I've got to hand it to you," he said. "I'm totally surprised that you're this open to a congenial arrangement. I thought you'd be ready to claw my eyes out."

The smile froze on her face and she couldn't seem to revive it. "You have to understand something." She sent him a flashing glance. "I'm open to congeniality because I'm hoping it redounds to my benefit. Nothing more. I want to be perfectly clear." She turned and held his gaze with her own steely version. "I want to keep this baby. I adore her. She's my life." Her voice choked but she pushed on, getting fiercer. "And she's mine. I will do anything I have to in order to keep her. Even claw your eyes out."

"Sara," he began, stepping toward her.

She held her hand up, stopping him.

"In the meantime, I want you to explore all the natural aspects of your paternal feelings. Go for it. Be a daddy for a day. Try your wings, so to speak."

He stared at her for a long moment, and then he started to laugh. "You're betting I'll punt, aren't you?"

She flushed. "I'm not betting on anything. I'm leaving it all up to you."

"Right." He shook his head, studying her more closely now. "Still waters run deep," he quoted. "I know you want me gone. I can understand that." He frowned thoughtfully. "Just don't try anything tricky, okay? Let's keep this struggle on the up-and-up."

She stared at him for a long moment, then nodded. "As you wish," she said crisply. "I'm not going to close any doors. I'm not going to be combative." She looked away, then swung around and stared at him again, hard. "But I am going to watch you like a hawk. Any chink in your armor will be duly noted."

He stared back, then gave her a lopsided grin. "Hey, you're on. May the best Mom win."

* * *

The park was filled with children. She glanced at Jake wondering how he was going to take all the high-pitched shrieking. It had taken her awhile to get used to it when she'd started out. The first few times she'd brought Savannah here, she'd thought her head would explode with all the frenetic noise. But he seemed to be taking it in stride, and when she tried saying something to him about it, he laughed.

"You should try living in a jungle when the monkeys start their daily chat," he said. "Now that will drive a grown man crazy in less than a day."

They found an empty bench at the outskirts of the younger children's playground. Sara held Savannah while Jake supervised the boys playing on the equipment and climbing through the playtime tunnels.

"Nice kids," he commented when he came back to sit beside her on the bench about half an hour later. The boys had followed him and were playing some sort of make-believe game in the sand in front of the bench.

"They're okay," she said modestly. After all, they were her nephews. But she couldn't help but wonder why they were so subdued today. And then she realized—it was because Jake was here and watching them. They knew a dominant male when they saw one.

Still, Tanner seemed to have a special charge of energy and pretty soon he was racing back and forth between the equipment and the bench, trying to organize all the other children into platoons. Timmy sat down on the sidewalk and began to make a sort of sand castle.

"We'd better keep an eye on them," she told Jake. "Tanner will end up starting a war if we're not careful."

Jake nodded and grinned. "No weapons, though," he noted.

"Oh, you just wait," she warned.

She pulled some plastic cups and bowls and shovels out of her carry-everything bag hanging from the stroller and gave them to Timmy to play with in the sand. She then put Savannah down beside him so that she could join in. The baby immediately began to pour sand from one container to another as though it was serious work that must be done.

Sara settled back and looked at Jake. He

was staring out toward the ocean, which was just visible through the trees.

"Tell me about Kelly," she said out of the blue.

He stiffened. "What do you want to know?"

Everything. Nothing. She took a deep breath. "Did you love her?"

He thought for a moment, then decided to tell the truth. "No."

She recoiled as though he'd said something awful.

"She didn't love me, either," he said quickly. "It wasn't like that. We met, we had a great time together and we both knew it was just for laughs."

Sara thought about that one for a moment, pursing her lips. "How do you know for sure that she felt that way, too?"

He shook his head. "You can tell. I've known enough women in my time to know the signs. She said as much and I believed her. She knew the score, and so did I. We were a perfect match, but it was temporary."

Sara looked away and made a face. She'd been hoping for a more romantic story. "So what happened?"

"We met at a party in Waikiki. We hit it off right away. I was in Hawaii for a couple of weeks of R and R. She was scoping out the job market, thinking of making the islands her home for a while. We got together and spent two weeks seeing the sights, swimming, eating fabulous food. We had a great time."

She searched his blue eyes. "So you liked her."

"Sure. I liked her quite a bit." He grimaced and tried to explain a bit more fully. "Listen, Sara, I've never been the marrying kind. I never expected to have a child. I thought I was being careful to make sure that didn't happen, and then, all of a sudden, there it was."

"There it was," she repeated softly, looking down at Savannah. Her sweet, sweet baby. What if she was really his? She bit her lip. She wasn't going to cry in front of him. Instead she rose, picked up Savannah and talked a bit of silly nonsense to her, then gazed at the playing children. She frowned.

"Wait a minute. Where's Tanner?"

Jake stood up beside her and shaded his eyes, surveying the scene. "I don't see him."

He looked again and shook his head. "He's gone."

"What? He can't be."

Fear shook her, but she held it off. She searched again. He had to be there somewhere.

"Isn't there another area over the hill?" Jake asked.

"Yes, the play equipment for the older kids. But…" Could Tanner have gone there? He never had before. Still, if not there, where?

Her heart began to beat like a drum. "Oh, why wasn't I watching? Where did he go?"

"Would he have started for home on his own?"

She whirled and looked down the street. "I don't think so. And we should be able to see him. We can see all the way down to the corner."

Her breath was coming in gasps now.

She turned and thrust her baby into Jake's arms. "Here, hold Savannah. I've got to find him."

He seemed startled, not sure of what to do with the baby. "But, wait…"

She raced over to where Timmy was playing. "Timmy, where's Tanner? Do you know where he went?"

Timmy just stared up at her with huge eyes as though he didn't have a clue what she was asking him.

"Oh!" She didn't wait. "Watch the kids," she called back to Jake. And then she ran.

She'd learned from the first when she helped take care of the twins that losing sight of a child was one of the worse experiences you could have. The panic that started pushing its way up her throat was wrenching.

"Oh, please, please, please," she muttered in her own simple prayer that he might be okay—okay and found soon. "Oh, please!"

He wasn't near the preschool slides, nor the close-by junior merry-go-round. He wasn't at the bounce house.

"Have you seen a little two year old with a blue Danny Duck cape on?" she began to ask everyone she passed. "Reddish hair. Blue eyes."

All she got were shrugs and apologies.

"Sorry. Haven't seen him."

She knew it was fruitless. He was just like twenty other boys his age playing here. Her heart was beating hard and she ran past the rocky stream as she headed for the top of the hill.

And then she saw him. How on earth had he gone so far so fast? She'd reached the older kids playground with the heavy polished steel equipment as opposed to the soft, padded things the younger children dealt with. The pieces were huge and scary compared to what they were used to down the hill.

And there, at the top of the tallest, most dangerous-looking slide, sat Tanner, dangling his feet over the side and looking down as though he didn't have a care in the world.

"Tanner!" she cried, sinking to her knees in relief. "Oh, Tanner. There you are."

Rising again quickly, she began to race to the area beneath where he was.

"Tanner, wait! I'm coming."

He didn't look her way and the fear was coming back quickly. She reached the sandy area the slide was set in.

"Tanner," she called up. "Come on down, honey."

Tanner acted as though he'd never seen her before. He squinted his eyes. And then he rose, leaning under the bar and looking down on the wrong side of the slide.

"No!" She shaded her eyes against the sun. What was he doing? "No, Tanner. Come down the slide, sweetie. I'll catch you."

He bent over and looked down the slide, then he looked at her and shook his head.

"What's wrong? I'll help you. Come on, honey, we can do this."

He shook his head again, obviously scared to go down the big kid slide. And she could hardly blame him. It seemed so high! What little two-year-old would want to jump right into this crazy journey?

But paradoxically, he went to something even scarier. Instead of the slide, he turned back to the wrong side of the platform again and looked down at the sandy landing below. Sara's heart was in her throat again. It looked like—it couldn't be. But it was. The boy wanted to jump.

"No! Tanner, don't jump. It's too high."

He looked at her again, his eyes bright and shiny.

"Dandan Duck," he said happily, and he held out his arms so that his cape was ready to surge out behind him. He was going to try to fly down.

"No!" she yelled again, starting up the metal steps of the ladder to the top, going as fast as she could. She would never reach him in time. But she had to try. "Tanner, don't jump!"

"Dandan Duck!" he called back. He flapped his cape at her.

"No, Tanner," she called, climbing as fast as she could. She was almost there. "You can't fly. Stop!"

"I Dandan Duck."

And he stepped off the edge of the platform.

She screamed. She was terrified, barely clinging to the very top steps, leaning out as far as she could, as if she had a prayer of catching him. His small body fell past her, heading for the ground. She felt the earth begin to spin around her.

"No, no!" she cried desperately.

But then something happened. Everything went into slow motion, and there was Jake, down in the sand, holding Tanner.

He'd caught him! He'd caught him and he was already setting him down on the ground.

"Oh." She closed her eyes and everything went black. She lost her balance for just a moment, but that moment was long enough to make her lose her footing. The next thing she knew, she was falling, too. She grabbed at the railing, but it was too late.

She closed her eyes again, waiting for the jarring landing, praying she wasn't going to break anything. And she hit with a jarring thud, but not in the sand. Instead she found herself in Jake's arms, just like Tanner had.

She opened her eyes in surprise and stared up into his brilliant blue gaze. He was grinning.

"Wow, everybody's trying to fly today. What is it? A new trend?"

"Very cute," she managed to grate out. She struggled a bit, but he wasn't letting go. "Where's Tanner? Where's Savannah?"

"Everybody's right here," he said, turning so that she could see Savannah in the stroller and the twins sitting side by side on the cement walkway, their feet in the sand. Amazing. It seemed he'd taken care of everything.

She frowned, shaking her head as though

to clear it. "How did you do that so fast?" she asked accusingly.

"Magic," he teased. "Magic and fast footwork. I'm a trained rescuer, you know. We have our ways."

She searched his eyes and tried to catch her breath. She'd been through an emotional meat grinder for the last ten minutes and she hadn't gotten over it yet. It actually felt good to be in Jake's big strong arms, safe and unharmed. She was tempted to close her eyes and rest her head against his shoulder while her system recovered.

Jake was laughing at first. It all seemed so comical, catching one person after another that way. But there was something in those dark eyes....

His smile faded as their gazes caught and they stared at each other in a strange, twisted sort of wonder. The feel of her began to sink in. Her body felt warm and her shape felt rounded and provocative in his arms. Her skin was so soft and her scent so clean and sweet. Her lips were touched with pink and slightly swollen. There was a glazed look in her eyes.

Suddenly he wanted to kiss her more than anything in the world.

But that was nuts. If there was one thing he was not going to do it was get emotionally entangled with this woman. Kiss of death. He couldn't do it. And just like that—Savannah started to fuss, they pulled apart and he was snapped back to reality. He let her go, sliding to her feet, and they quickly backed away from each other.

It seemed like minutes had gone by, but it must have been only a few seconds. At least, she hoped so. She avoided looking at him again, embarrassed.

"Thanks for catching me," she muttered, busy with the clasp to Savannah's stroller. "And especially for catching Tanner. You lived up to your rescuer rep, I guess."

She glanced his way and found him frowning at her thoughtfully, as though what had just happened had given him food for thought.

He'd almost kissed her. She knew that. If the children hadn't been so close, he might have followed through. And to her horror, she also knew that for just a moment, she'd really wanted him to.

CHAPTER SIX

"LET'S GO," SARA said quickly, not wanting to talk about it any longer. She'd been hoping to catch Jake up in the difficulties of taking care of babies and she'd ended up being the one who hadn't coped all that well. He was the hero. And thank goodness he'd been there for them all.

"Time to go home."

They herded the children back and Jake was quite cheerful with them. She looked at him sharply, searching for evidence of getting tired or annoyed, but she didn't see any. That made her crosser than she normally was.

But they made it back to the house and then found themselves spending the next hour spinning their tales of adventure out for Jill and Connor and reenacting what they'd gone through—though they did skip most of the details concerning that spectacular last catch Jake had made.

The twins both told their parents all about it, one starting out the exposition and the other talking over him toward the end, beginning a new segment. They were so cute, but unfortunately, not a word of what they said was understandable. It was as though they spoke their own toddler language. But they were passionate and everyone gave them a good listen just the same, oohing and aahing over every incomprehensible detail.

"Is that right?" was repeated a lot. "Oh, my goodness." And that seemed to satisfy them. When it was over, they both looked very pleased with themselves.

Jill had fixed a nice lunch of grilled cheese sandwiches and tomato soup and the adults sat at the table while the children sat in pulled up high chairs. Sara gazed about the room as they ate, noting how Jake seemed to fit in much better than she'd expected. In fact, Jill and Connor obviously liked him a lot. They were talking and laughing with him as though they were old friends.

Why did that give her a hollow feeling in

the pit of her stomach? Why did she keep thinking of herself as the odd man out?

And then, when she was hoping it was time for Jake to go to his own house and leave them alone for the rest of the day, she heard Jill inviting him to the birthday party for the twins they were having the next day.

"Their second birthday," Jill was saying. "I know they'd love it if you could make it to help celebrate. We're just having a few friends over."

"I'd be honored to come," he said. "These two little guys are about as fun to hang out with as short people get."

Jill loved it. Sara watched her, feeling a bit resentful. She'd been looking forward to the birthday party and now she was going to have to share it with him.

Even worse, tomorrow was the last day before the DNA report was due. She was planning to try to talk him into reconsidering his plans to take over raising Savannah, but she needed more time. She hadn't done enough groundwork to convince him yet.

She needed to make it up as she went along. The first thing she did, once lunch was finished, was call Jake over and tell him it was time for a lesson in baby management.

"You might as well learn how to do some of these things," she told him. "You might end up having to take over. Let's see if you're a quick study."

He seemed nervous. "What exactly are you talking about here?"

"Changing diapers. Giving a baby a bath. Putting her down for her nap. Dealing with her when she cries. Reading her favorite books to her. Keeping her busy and in a learning environment at the same time. Singing songs. Walking her when she needs to be carried." She shook her head. "I could go on and on. I just think you ought to get some taste of what you're signing up for."

"Of course. You're right."

He said the words, but he still looked more uncertain than she'd ever seen him look before. She smiled. Maybe this was going to be effective after all.

"Okay," she said. "You pick her up and bring her this way. We'll take her up to the room where she's staying."

"Pick her up?" he said, frowning.

"You managed at the park," she reminded him.

He nodded. "Sure. I can do that."

And he did. But he appeared scared to death for the first few moments. She smiled again. Then he began to hold Savannah like a real, live baby instead of a fragile and oddly shaped potato, and her smile dimmed a bit. He seemed to be catching on awfully fast.

"Okay, here's the deal," she told him quickly. "I'll walk you through everything today. Tomorrow you come in the morning and you'll do it all again, only this time, you'll be on your own. Got it?"

He nodded.

"How long did it take you to get up to speed?" he asked as they negotiated the stairs and headed into the upper bedroom.

"What are you talking about?" she shot back.

"Come on. You say you took care of your sister's boys so you know all about babies, but I don't believe it. I'll bet there was still a lot you had to learn."

She closed her eyes for a moment, thinking. She remembered her resolution—casual conversation, not confrontation. She was a lot more likely to get somewhere if he thought they were talking on a friendly basis. Honesty seemed the best option for her anyway.

"It was pretty hard at first," she admitted. "That was why we stayed here with Jill for the first week. She was there to help me over the rough spots."

She gestured for him to lay the baby down on the changing table and he complied fairly gracefully, then smiled down at the sweet little girl who grinned back at him and waved her arms, reaching for his fingers whenever they got close.

"So you would recommend having someone there with me at first?" he asked.

It was a simple question. She should have been able to handle it. But for some reason, resentment shot through her and she flushed. "What are you asking me? Advice on what to do when you steal my baby?"

He turned and stared at her. "Come on, Sara. It's not like that."

She couldn't help it. Suddenly it was all too real and menacing. "Yes, it is like that."

She turned away so that she wouldn't be

actually glaring at him. Using every ounce of strength, she made herself calm down. "And yes, I would recommend very strongly that you have someone onboard who knows what she's doing. Probably someone full-time, because you're a man and men always seem to have things they have to do away from the house." She turned back and met his gaze rather defiantly. "And I certainly don't expect you to learn how to sit around rocking the cradle, so to speak."

He stared at her but he didn't say a thing and she flushed even redder, wishing she had held her tongue. She watched as he steeled himself for the job.

"Okay," he said quietly. "Tell me what to do. I'm ready."

He did great. Of course, he had her there to give him advice every step of the way. But she had to admit, he didn't waver. He watched as she changed Savannah's diaper. He was still hesitant to try that on his own. But he did walk her, humming a sweet song to help her go to sleep and then he lay her down gently in her little bed and she sighed and went right off to dreamland.

"How'd I do?" he whispered, looking pleased with himself as they made their way downstairs.

She nodded, feeling sad and lost. "You did just fine. Really. I'm impressed."

His grin could have lit up the sky. He took her hand and regarded her candidly.

"Hey, Sara," he said. "Thanks for today. I know it was hard for you to let me be a part of it. It must have cut into your heart to let me be this close to Savannah for so long. But you know what?" His grin was genuine and disarming. "This was one of the best days of my life."

And he walked off down the driveway, whistling as he went.

Sara stayed where she was, tears running down her face. There was no way she could spin this. He was basically a pretty good guy. She wanted to hate him, but even that had been taken away from her.

Sara went to her room and spent another hour in agony before she could get the tears to stop. She was very scared, but she couldn't let that stop her from moving forward with her plan to prove to Jake that he just wasn't father material. At least, not single father material.

Savannah was down for the night but it was still light outside. She decided to run over to take a look at the progress the workers had made on her house. She knew she'd been neglecting it lately. Other things had been on her mind.

She drove up, parked in front and went inside. It looked like her addition was almost completed. They were still working on the new bathroom, but it was gorgeous.

All the workmen had gone home for the night. She'd lived in this house for a number of years, but it had a strange, lonely feeling now that Savannah wasn't filling the place with love and laughter. If she lost her baby, would she be able to live here? She wasn't sure. It would be painful.

The new bedroom for Savannah was beautiful, powder-pink with white trim. She'd already begun furnishing it with a new crib and changing table. It was beautiful. The question was, would it ever be used by the little girl it was meant for?

She bit her lip and forced back the hopeless feelings. She was going to keep fighting so there was no use letting pessimism build up and handicap her spirits. She was going to win this.

She looked out the window toward the neighbor's house that Jake was renting. She'd heard music as she'd walked up to her own house. There seemed to be people visiting him. Noisy people. There was something going on.

Two huge Harley-Davidson motorcycles sat in the front, pulled onto the grass. What kind of people was he having over, anyway? It was none of her business. But she had to know.

No. She closed her eyes and took a deep breath and thought better of it. She had nothing to talk to him about that couldn't wait until morning. She would get into her car and drive away and leave it alone.

Sure she would.

She gave it a try. She walked to her car and opened the door and then someone shouted something borderline vulgar and she turned and made a beeline toward his front door.

A large jovial man answered the bell. He leaned out toward her appreciatively.

"Hey," he greeted. "You here for the party?"

"What party?" she snapped with disapproval.

"Oops. I guess not." He backed away, looking chagrined. "Sounds like a disgruntled neighbor to me. Help."

Jake came into the room and headed straight for the door. "Sara. What is it? Is there something wrong?"

"No." She frowned at him. "I was just checking out my house next door and I heard the music, so I thought I'd check out what was going on."

She glanced past him and saw two other large men filling up the couches. "So you're having a party?" she asked skeptically.

"Absolutely not," he told her. He looked back at the others. "Would you like to come in and meet my friends?" he asked, though he didn't look as though he really wanted her to. "They're guys who served with me in the Army."

"No." She shook her head. "Oh, no. I don't want to intrude. I just…" She shrugged helplessly.

He grinned and came out to join her on the porch, closing the door behind him.

A burst of laughter came from inside the house. Sara frowned. "Was that man on the couch the man from the other night?" she asked.

"My buddy Starman. That was him."

"What are they here for?" she asked.

"They just want me to join them on a little pleasure cruise," he said, his mouth twisting.

"What?" she asked, puzzled.

He sighed. "I was being sarcastic. They've got a project going, a quasi-military operation they think I should join them in. A sort of revenge plot off in the jungles of Southeast Asia."

Sara shook her head emphatically. "You can't do that."

He looked surprised. "I can't?"

"Of course not." Here it was, custom made for her purposes. He had to face the fact that taking possession of a baby would make all the difference. He had to come to terms with that before he tore all their lives apart.

He was shaking his head. "That's a knee-jerk reaction. You don't know what it's all about."

"No, I don't. But I do know that you can't go."

He frowned, looking almost angry. "Really?"

"Yes. If the DNA comes in as you expect it to, you can't go. You're Savannah's father now. You're not a lone wolf warrior type anymore. You've got a responsibility to your baby."

He blinked and raked fingers through his hair. "I understand that. And believe me, it's not easy. I've got things tugging at me in more than one direction right now."

She reached out to touch him. It happened so naturally, she didn't realize what she was doing until it was too late.

"I can see that you're torn," she told him, her hand on his chest. She gazed earnestly into his blue eyes. "But you have to understand that Savannah has to be your first priority. She's the most important thing in the world. To both of us."

He raised his own hand and covered hers, but he was watching her in a strange way, as though he didn't quite get where she was coming from. And in truth, she didn't get it, either. Savannah was either his or hers. She couldn't have it both ways. Could she?

"Don't worry," he said, his voice husky with some raw emotion she couldn't quite place. "I understand how important she is. Believe me. I understand."

Something special passed between them, something human, a connection she'd never had with anyone before. It sent a thrill through her, but it sent a warning shiver as well. She and Jake had strings between them that could never completely be cut. It was very strange, but it was real.

"I'd better go," she said, pulling her hand away and looking toward the ocean. "I…I just wanted to stop by and…well, I was looking at the progress at my house."

"Oh," he said, following her to her car. "How does it look?"

"Great. You'll have to come over and see it soon."

"I'd like to."

She tried to smile at him. "I guess we'll see you tomorrow at the birthday party."

"Sure."

She nodded, got into her car and left. Looking in her rearview mirror, she could see him standing there, watching her go.

Jake was back first thing in the morning, out on a swing in the backyard again. Jill thought it was cute. Sara thought it was obnoxious. Connor didn't have an opinion.

"Do we have anymore of that Praline Rum Cake?" he asked instead of dwelling on it. "That would make a spectacular breakfast."

Jill smiled and mussed his hair. "I know. And that's why you're not getting any. Oatmeal for you, darling."

"What?"

"Somebody's got to keep an eye on your waistline."

"My waistline is doing fine," he grumbled, but he knew better than to push it.

Sara put on a jacket and went out. There was a cool breeze coming off the ocean. She marched out to where Jake sat, doing all she could not to respond to his wide smile.

"Where's my girl?" he said.

Sara gave him a look. "She's still asleep. You're early."

"Oh." His grin was sheepish. "Sorry about that. I'm so in love with that kid, I just can't stay away."

She stared at him. Here he was, casually planning to rip her heart from her body, and he didn't seem to know how offensive he was. If he kept this up, she would find it easy to hate him.

"Hey, I brought something you might want to see," he said, and he reached into his jacket and pulled out a set of four photos and handed them to her. "Pictures I took of Kelly during those two weeks in Waikiki."

She pored at them, startled to see her half sister smiling at the camera. She was so pretty and looked so alive. It was hard to believe...

"Oh!" she said. "I've got to show these to Jill."

He nodded, then rose and followed her back to the house.

Sara held the pictures out to her sister without saying a word, and within seconds, both women were crying. He looked away. He was tortured about it, too, but he didn't have any tears for Kelly.

That didn't mean he wasn't sorry she'd died.

Of course he was. It was a horrible tragedy. And he had to admit there was a thread of remorse in his recollections of her. Kelly wasn't a bad memory—unfortunately, she wasn't much of a memory at all.

She was a fun date for a few days, and once he'd left Hawaii, he hadn't really thought about her again until he got back to the States from overseas and prison camp and found all the letters she'd sent. The pictures really didn't do much to bring her back to him in any meaningful way.

He tried to think if there was any way Sara looked at all like Kelly. He couldn't see it. Or maybe he just didn't remember exactly what Kelly looked like—beyond the pictures.

Wait. Yes, there was one thing—her smile. Kelly had been blessed with a smile that drew people in. It made you want to share in her happiness. Sara's smile had been a lot like that at first. But he hadn't seen that radiance return once she'd known his identity. Would he ever see it again? Funny, but he wanted to.

It was a good thing the birthday party had been scheduled for afternoon, because Sara and Jill were emotionally wiped out for hours after seeing the pictures of Kelly.

"I'll never forgive myself for not having reached out to her more strongly," Jill said, tears in her eyes. "We should have brought her here. We should have made an effort to get to know her so much better than we did. I always thought we would, someday. And now it's too late."

"What do you think was behind it?" Sara mused, wiping away her own tears. "Why did we tend to have that lingering, simmering resentment of Kelly?"

Jill thought for a moment, then offered, "I think it was because of what she represented. She was our father's child with the woman who came to take our mother's place. We focused all our grief on her and we hated them both. It wasn't fair, but we did."

"I can't believe we did that. We were older. We should have known better. If we'd stopped and thought things through, if we'd stepped back and looked at the bigger picture…"

Jill hugged Sara and sighed. "But we never did. You just go on in life, so often, just taking day by day and not looking outward."

Sara frowned, thinking it over. What Jill had said still bothered her. "Hate is too strong a word, don't you think?" she ventured.

Jill hesitated, then nodded. "You're right. But we couldn't stand that woman. She tried to take our mother's place, and she was so bossy and unfriendly to us. And she didn't treat Daddy very well at all."

"Which is why their marriage didn't last."

"True." Jill managed a bittersweet smile. "Remember how we celebrated with hot fudge sundaes the day he told us they were separating?"

Sara nodded. "Yes. We must have been about fourteen and fifteen at the time. We were so happy the evil stepmother was gone." She sighed, shaking her head. "But that meant we never got to know Kelly very well, beyond her toddler years."

"Yes. It's such a pity."

"And that was part of why I decided to take Savannah when they asked us if we would. To try to make up—at least a little bit—for not being kinder to Kelly."

Jill groaned. "And now you may have to pay the price for us both."

"Oh, don't say that!" Sara said, hands to her mouth.

They stared into each other's eyes and both looked tragic and filled with remorse. Sara pulled Jill aside to where they could speak privately.

"You realize what this means, don't you?" she whispered to her sister. "These pictures prove he knew her and was with her right at the appropriate time. Look at the date stamp on the photos."

Jill nodded. "I noticed," she said. "Oh, Sara. What are we going to do?"

Sara's jaw tightened. "Convince him he doesn't really want to be a father," she said. "Unless you can think of something better."

Connor saw the way the wind was blowing and he asked Jake if he wanted to go along with him to the hardware store. He was looking for a new tool to use in making a tree house for the boys. Jake jumped at the chance to leave the agonizing behind. They talked about sports and cars and tools and had a great time, returning quite happy and refreshed, carrying a nice shiny new power screwdriver set.

Mrs. Truesdale, from the agency, called while they were gone. She deeply commiserated with Sara and promised to do all she could from her end of things.

"I know I have to be impartial," she told her. "But I put you together with your baby and I would hate to see that slip away. You are so perfect for it." Her voice was lower, almost secretive. "Now you keep track of anything that seems strange to you. Good documentation is important. I've often seen it win the day. And don't worry, I'll be in touch. We'll work on this together."

Sara was feeling a bit better after that conversation. She and Jill had pretty much gone through their catharsis by the time the men got back and were ready to move on with their day. It was time to start preparing for the party.

There was plenty to do, games to be set up, food to be prepared, play areas to be set out. Most of the children attending would be toddlers themselves, so the games would be completely basic and simple. Still, they needed to be thought through. Everyone was helping.

"Except for you," Sara told Jake. "I have something special saved for you."

He turned to look at her, his smile crooked and rather endearing. "Special for me, huh? Great. What do you want me to do?"

She stood watching him with her hands on her hips, wishing he didn't look like every woman's dream of the perfect guy. It would be easier to fight a man who gave you the willies instead of butterflies in the tummy area. "You're going to be a nanny for Savannah."

He frowned. "What exactly does that mean? I thought I did that yesterday."

"No, you just mostly observed yesterday. Today you'll be hands-on and on your own. Your job is to watch her. Help her when she gets stuck. Find her something to play with. Hold her. Change her when she needs it. Rock her when she cries. Feed her when she needs it. Put her down for a nap when she gets cranky."

Jake looked out toward where Connor was setting up the plywood clown panels for the sponge throwing game. "But I could be helping with the building crew," he noted wistfully. "I'm pretty good with a hammer."

"No time," she said blithely. "You're going to be in charge of Savannah's health and happiness." She smiled at him. "I'll be watching."

"Great," he said halfheartedly, but he didn't argue. He knew that Sara had a double reason for wanting him to take on this challenge and he agreed with at least one of them. He had to learn this stuff. Having someone who'd been doing it for six months give him pointers was extremely useful and he couldn't waste that resource.

The second reason she was doing it was not quite as clear, but he thought he'd figured it out pretty quickly. She was hoping he would do a lousy job at it and get frustrated. Was she trying to make him feel like a loser? No, he really didn't think so. But she did want him to feel like this job was too big for him to handle. Well, maybe not too big, but too far out of his bailiwick. She wanted him to realize that it would be harder than he'd thought.

He had to admit he'd already had a few qualms along those lines. After all, the dream of having a child of his own was very different from the reality of actually dealing with one. He knew it was going to be hard. There was nothing easy about taking on responsibility for another human being, especially one that needed constant attention and care. He wasn't particularly talented in that direction and he'd had no experience. But he also knew that the connection he felt with Savannah was pure and clear and unique. He'd never known anything like it. And now that he'd felt it, he knew he couldn't walk away, no matter what.

Okay, he would do it. He would act as a nanny and let Sara judge his talents. Why not? Anything for his little girl.

"I really do appreciate the effort you're putting into this, Sara," he said. "Believe me, the reality of this had hit me like a slap in the face. It's a whole different way of looking at the world when you've suddenly got someone else to think about. Someone who depends on you. I've never had that before."

Good, she thought, nodding in response. Another piece of ammunition. She had to file that away for future use. She would have to start making lists and keeping track of the things he said. This was war and she had to stay focused. Any sign of weakness was a point for her side.

She began preparing sandwiches for the kids, but she was keeping her eye on Jake's progress at the same time. She watched as he patiently fed her one of the sandwiches, making each bite zoom in like an airplane to make her laugh. When she was finished, he cleaned her up and found a toy and played with her for half an hour. By then, it was pretty obvious she needed changing.

Sara followed the two of them as they climbed the stairs to the room. Jake was looking very brave and determined. Savannah was happy in his arms. Sara followed and hung out in the doorway, just in case. He lay her down on the changing table and tugged off her jumper, then stared at the diaper for a long moment. He looked over at Sara and made a face.

"Maybe I ought to watch you do it one more time," he said.

She smiled. That was exactly the reaction she'd been hoping for. "Sure," she said, stepping up and taking over. "Why not?"

Once she'd put on a new diaper, she handed her baby over to Jake again. "Now pick out some clothes to put on her," she said. "On a nice late summer day like this, what would you choose?"

He stared at her, completely at sea. "Give me a hint," he said.

She grinned. "A sundress over tights. How about that?"

"Great." He looked at the open drawer and hesitated. "What exactly are tights again?" he asked.

She laughed and showed him, then guided him away from the purple leggings he was about to put on Savannah. "Try to find something that will go with her green dress," she suggested.

She watched as he finished dressing her. She liked the way he talked to her, half teasing, half loving. The way he looked, the tone of his voice, the expression in his eyes, touched her heart. He really did love that little girl. She could see that. This was going to be tough.

"All in all, you're doing quite well," she told him as he swung his baby up into his arms again. "I'm impressed."

Then she bit her lip. What was she doing praising him? She wanted him to feel inade-

quate, didn't she? Wasn't that the whole point?
She had to be more careful. This was war and
she couldn't give up ground too easily.

For the next hour as she watched him with
Savannah, her mood darkened. He did things
wrong and she pointed them out as they happened, but he learned quickly and the way he
treated Savannah, his growing attachment to
her couldn't be more clear.

Sara was losing all hope. He was her father
and the only way she was going to be able to
fight that would be to talk him out of wanting to take over her parenting. Was there any
chance she could do that? She couldn't think
about it too hard, not if she wanted to keep
functioning for the rest of the day.

But her face told the story and Jake noticed. He'd just put Savannah down for her
nap and was feeling pretty good about how
things had gone when he caught sight of Sara.
She'd slipped away and was standing in the
den, looking out at the ocean in the distance.
He came up behind her and touched her arm.
She whirled and gazed up at him, tears standing in her eyes.

He took hold of her shoulders and frowned. "Hey, what happened? What's the matter?"

She shook her head, trying to avoid his gaze. "Nothing."

His hands tightened on her shoulders. "Come on. You can tell me."

She glanced up into his eyes, then away again. "I'm…I'm just upset."

"About what?"

She shook her head.

"Come on, Sara. If I've done something…"

"No." She took a deep breath. "It's not you. It's me." She took another breath and blurted out, "I really, really want to hate you. And I can't."

"Oh."

She was crying now. She hated that he was there to see it, but she couldn't stop. His arms came around her and he held her close, letting her sob against his chest, murmuring soft words of reassurance that she hardly heard. But she felt his comfort, and she relaxed within it, wishing…wishing…

No. She had to stop this. She forced herself to regain her balance and get back to her normal independent self. She couldn't show him this sort of silliness. She pulled away and gave him a watery smile.

"I...I'm just tired, that's all," she said, turning away. "I've got to get back to the kitchen. Jill needs help." And she escaped.

Jake stayed where he was for a few minutes, swearing softly and running his fingers through his thick hair. It wasn't often that he felt sympathy for another quite so strongly. But he could imagine what it would be like to be Sara and put in this position. It wasn't pretty.

He'd had his own moments of doubt, but that was over now. The better he got to know Savannah, the more sure he was. She was his and he had to take care of her. It was that simple.

CHAPTER SEVEN

FINALLY IT WAS party time, and for the most part, things went great. Friends of Jill and Connor began to stream in, most of them trailed by toddlers on their chubby, shaky legs. Sara watched them come and hid a smile. It was definitely a day for the short people of the island. Children under five seemed to rule the roost.

That meant noise, lots of noise, once the beginning shyness wore off and the children were playing in the backyard. Moms and dads hovered at the margins, rushing in to settle disputes or kiss an owwie.

Most were friends of Jill's that Sara didn't know very well. She helped organize games and supply party favors. The food Jill had spread out on the tables was super yummy and Sara took pity on Jake about an hour in, telling him she'd watch Savannah while he ate and did a little socializing.

She was just helping Savannah onto a rocking horse in the playroom when a friend of her sister's, a woman named Mary Ellen, stopped in to chat.

Mary Ellen had a bouffant blond hair helmet, scarlet fingernails and a roving eye. The first thing she wanted to know was all about Jake.

"Okay, Sara," she said, giving her an air kiss and then standing back to look at her. "I understand that delicious man in the tight jeans is a friend of yours. What exactly does that mean?"

Sara bristled a bit. She'd never been all that fond of Mary Ellen. "What do you think it means?"

She shrugged. "I just want to know if you've got dibs on him, or is he fair game?"

Sara looked at her, chin high, eyes narrowed. This woman wanted Jake. How dare she?

And yet, she had to admit, Jake was a free man and she had no claim on him whatsoever. Still, Mary Ellen didn't have to know that.

"And if he is?" she asked. "Just exactly what are you planning?"

Mary Ellen looked out the picture window to where Jake was standing talking to some of the others and watching the children play.

"A lady never reveals her secrets, my dear." She laughed to show that was just a joke. "Oh, nothing. Everybody knows I'm hopelessly devoted to Hector. But a girl can dream, you know."

She winked as though the two of them had an understanding about these things.

If this woman doesn't stop, I'm going to throw up! Sara silently screamed. She had a sudden vision of Jake dating someone like Mary Ellen while raising Savannah and it sent a wave of sick agony through her. She would do almost anything to stop that from ever happening.

"Too bad," she said sharply. "Better luck next time."

"Oh." Mary Ellen looked disappointed. "So you *are* actually dating him, are you?"

"Yes, I am," she lied. But what could she do? The woman deserved what she got. "He and I have a very special understanding."

"Ah." Mary Ellen had no idea what that meant, but she accepted it with good grace and beat a hasty retreat toward the backyard. Straight to Jake, Sara noticed. He would have a good laugh when she told him about the "special relationship" the two of them supposedly had, but she couldn't help that now. Oh, well.

Still, it did point out a factor to be considered. Jake was attractive to women. If he took Savannah, there would be women, and maybe, eventually, a special woman. And no matter how many visitation plans Sara might have, it wouldn't last. If she thought anything along those lines might work, she was dreaming.

Savannah was getting fussy. She wanted to go back outside where the action was. Sara pulled her up into her arms and carried her out, and she found herself standing just behind where Jake was talking to another guest she didn't know.

"I hear you've been deployed in Southeast Asia for the last few years," the man, who she thought was a friend of Connor's, was saying to him.

Jake paused as though this was a topic he

really didn't relish getting into. "You might call it that," he said at last. "I was definitely in the area."

The man nodded wisely. "Something tells me that means you may have spent some quality time at the Mekrob Mansion. Am I right?"

She'd heard that name before. It seemed to her she'd seen it in news reports. She had a vague impression that is wasn't a very nice place.

"I've heard it called that." Jake seemed to shiver slightly. "What a benign name for the reality of that place."

"I had a buddy who spent some time there," the friend told him. "He came out a changed man, pretty much a shell of the person he used to be."

"I've had friends who had similar experiences," Jake said, starting to turn away. "Luckily I seem to be able to heal faster than most." And he began to make his way to the food table.

Sara watched him go, feeling sick. She knew he'd had a rough time over the last few years. He'd hinted at it often enough. But just how rough was it? She wasn't sure she really wanted to know the details.

She carried Savannah over to where the children were playing so that she could watch without getting too involved. Friends of Jill's stopped to talk to her and to admire her little girl. She loved showing her off. With her lively smile and her curly yellow hair, she looked great no matter what she wore.

Sara held Savannah close, trying not to think about how fast the time was going. In just a few hours, the agency would call and hand out the verdict. She was pretty sure she already knew what it would be. She looked down at her baby's beautiful face and sang her a soft song. She had to treasure every moment, just in case.

Savannah's legs began to kick and she pointed, laughing. Sara looked at the direction she was pointing in. Jake was helping to erect a piece of plywood with the figure of a clown painted on it, with a round cutout where the face should be. He looked through the hole and wiggled his eyebrows at Savannah.

It was time for the wet sponges!

This had to be the children's favorite game.

Even two-year-olds could manage tossing a wet sponge. And when they had a target like Jake, making faces and pretending to be hit even when he wasn't, the laughter never stopped.

Savannah was still too young for this, but she laughed and laughed seeing Jake take the punishment from the other children. At one point, Sara put a wet sponge in her hand and took her right up to the clown form and let her press it to his nose.

He yelled as though it was his worse wound yet and Savannah turned red with laughter. Sara's gaze met Jake's and his eyes were filled with fun and happiness. She smiled. She couldn't help it.

Still, the feeling of dread was always there at the back of her mind. The time of reckoning was at hand.

By the time Jake had finished his turn in the target zone, he was drenched.

"Come on in," Jill said, guiding him into the kitchen, where Savannah was playing with balloons with two older children on the carpeted area of the floor. "Connor will let you use one of his shirts. Sara will show you where they are."

"Okay," he said, still laughing as he pulled a pack of breath mints out of his shirt pocket. The cardboard packaging was ruined and he spilled the mints out onto the coffee table so they wouldn't be ruined, too, and then he threw away the box.

Sara was already heading up the stairs and he followed her, pulling off the wet shirt as he went. She avoided looking at his beautiful chest as she took his wet shirt and traded it for one of Connor's, but as he turned, for the first time, she got a good look at his back in full light and gasped at what she saw.

There was a crisscross pattern of scarring all up and down the surface. The first thing that came to mind was the evidence left of a lashing. The long purple welts tipped in red looked awfully recent to her and she felt sick.

"What is that?" she cried before she thought.

He glanced in the mirror, saw what she was looking at and quickly pulled his shirt on all the way.

"Just a little memento of my prison camp

days," he said lightly. "Don't give it a second thought."

She stared at him, hand to her throat. "I overheard you talking to that man in the yard," she said, her voice strained. "So you were at the Mekrob Mansion?"

"Sara, you don't want to hear about it. Believe me. It's in my past and I don't even think about it much anymore. No problem."

No problem. Someone with scarring like that had to be affected in more ways than just the physical. She couldn't believe she hadn't noticed it before. But then, she'd spent a lot of time studiously trying to avoid looking at his naked torso, as if she thought it would have magic powers over her if she let herself gaze too long. And who knew? Maybe it did.

But somehow, now that she'd seen them and actually brought the scarring up to him, she couldn't seem to let them go.

"Jake, they don't look that old to me. Are you sure you're psychologically ready to take care of a child with that sort of damage done to you so recently?"

He looked at her for a second, then grinned, shaking his head. "Oh, yeah. I think I can handle it." Reaching out, he took her chin in his hand and smiled down at her. "Now you're clutching at straws, Sara. Cut it out."

She flushed but she didn't look away. Sure she was clutching at straws. She would try anything to win this fight. She wasn't the least bit embarrassed.

As they came back down the stairs, the first thing Sara saw was Savannah turning purple and making choking sounds, writhing on the floor, a sight that sent a shock of horror flashing through her. There was no adult in sight and the two children she'd been playing with were just going out the sliding glass door.

"Savannah!" she screamed, rushing to her. Somehow, Jake beat her to the child and had her in his arms, holding her from behind and pressing in the right place to get a burping sound out of her. Two breath mints came shooting out of her mouth, and just like that, she was breathing again.

Jill came in at the same time. "I just went out for a second," she cried, seeing what was going on. "Really! No more than a second. How did this happen so fast?"

But it wasn't Jill who Sara blamed.

"Who left those out where she could get them?" she demanded, sweeping the rest of them up in her hand.

"I did," Jake admitted. "I didn't think..."

"You didn't think!" She glared at him, anger hot and painful all through her body. Her baby, her little child, what if they hadn't found her in time? What if she'd died, or had brain damage, or some other horror? What if?

"How could you do that? You didn't think! She could have died if we hadn't come back in time!"

Jake's face went hard as stone. "I should have known better. Sorry. It won't happen again."

"Sorry!" Sara wanted to shake him. She was almost sputtering with her anger. "Sorry! What good is 'sorry' when..."

"Sara." Jill grabbed her hand and pulled her around as though to silence her. "Enough. She's okay. Jake will know better next time. Give it a rest."

Meanwhile, Savannah was back to normal. She'd reached up and put her arms around Jake's neck and she was babbling to him, non-sense words, but the meaning was clear. She might as well have been saying, "Thank you, Daddy. You saved my life."

Sara turned away in frustration. She was trembling with fear and anger. She glanced back at where Jake held Savannah, and she turned and headed up the stairs again, going to her own room and hoping to calm down once she was alone for a few minutes.

Jake watched her go. A black cloud loomed over him. How could he have done that, without thinking? It hadn't occurred to him—but that was the point, wasn't it? There was so much he had to learn—so much that didn't come naturally to him as yet. It wasn't going to be easy.

And Sara was right to yell at him. He deserved it. If his lack of care and knowledge did anything to hurt this adorable child in his arms, he would never forgive himself. This parenting thing was going to require a lot of work. Was he really ready to take it on?

The party was finally over. Large hunks of cake and dabs of frosting were littered all over the backyard, but the squirrels would get what

Sara and Jill didn't get swept up. The men were putting away the tools and the plywood characters and the game structures that had been set up around the yard. Jill put away the leftover food and Sara tried to put the twins down. She soon gave up. They were much too excited from the party and all their new toys to think about something so boring as sleep.

Jake was holding Savannah. He'd been holding her almost continuously ever since the breath mint incident, as though constant apologies were needed for now. Sara watched and felt her anger drain away. How could she be mad at someone who loved her baby as much as she did—regardless of the consequences?

"I'm going to talk to him," Sara told her sister once the worst of the devastation had been cleaned up and they were outside, surveying the scene.

Jake was inside, holding Savannah. She could see him through the sliding glass door. Jill turned and looked at him, too.

"I'm going to confront him with what his life will be like and how he ought to leave the raising of Savannah to me."

Jill nodded, her eyes shadowed with sorrow. "Good luck," she said softly.

Sara went in to the room where he sat with the sleepy girl up against his shoulder and sank onto the ottoman in front of his chair.

"Jake, I need to talk to you." She was ready. Her heart was thumping. She had to do it now. There was no time left for avoiding this. The agency would be calling in the morning and by then, everything would be too crazy to get a serious conversation in.

"Is she asleep?" he asked softly.

Sara craned to see her face and looked at her eyes. They were closed. "I think so," she told him.

He smiled. "She feels asleep," he said, half whispering. "I can't tell you how much I love holding her like this."

That touched her heart. How could it not?

"Here, let me take her. I want to put her down in her play bed. That'll keep her out of the line of fire for now." She settled the baby in the soft playpen, covered her with a blanket and turned back to Jake.

"I have to say something to you," she began,

sitting back down on the ottoman. "I know you're not going to like it. But I have to say it."

He raised his gaze to hers and looked serious. "Go."

She drew air in deeply and began. "I want Savannah. I love her. I'm her mother. Please, please don't take her away from me."

He stared at her, then shook his head. "You're not going to like what I have to say, either," he warned. "Sara, I'm her father. And... you're not really her mother—you're her aunt. I have a more fundamental right to her than you do. It's that simple."

She drew in a shaky breath and held her head high. "No, it's not that simple. I'm a woman. I've learned how to nurture this child. You're a man. Your place in the scheme of things is very different. I know you love her. It's obvious. And she loves you. I'm not saying I want to tear that apart. I'm just saying, we each have our roles, and yours isn't to be her mother."

His blue eyes narrowed. "But yours is."

"Yes." She said it firmly. She wanted him to see how committed she was to this plan. "Yes, I really think so."

He shook his head. "Sara…"

"Hear me out. Jake, you're wonderful with Savannah. You're gentle and kind and good to her. But you're still a man. And she needs a woman to help her become one herself. There are a thousand different ways a girl needs a mother."

His frown became fierce. "That's nonsense."

"No. It's truth. You've spent the day taking care of her. Do you want to do the same thing again tomorrow?"

He grimaced dismissively. "What does that mean?"

"I'm trying to get you to think through what it means to raise a little girl. You have to watch her every moment. You have to be there for her for eighteen years, at least. You have to be her support in so many ways."

"I can do that."

"Yes, but alone? I don't think you realize how hard it will be."

"I can do it. I can." He glared at her. "No matter what, I can't walk away. That's not going to happen."

"Of course not." She touched him, putting her hand on his arm. She wanted him to see that she wasn't the enemy here. She wanted to be sure she kept open all lines of communication. "You're her biological father. You have to be a part of her life. But..."

"I know what you're saying, Sara. I understand traditional ways. Even though I wasn't raised that way, we all pretty much have that baked in the cake, don't we? But extraordinary things happen, and we have to make do. I'm adaptable. I'm ready to adapt to being a single father." He shook his head and stared into her eyes, emotion clear and determined. "I can't think of anything I want more."

She pulled her hand back. So far, she couldn't detect one gap in his armor, one area of vulnerability in his logic. She'd attacked and he hadn't retreated one bit. Was there really any hope lurking in there behind those brilliant blue eyes?

"How about money?" she challenged. It was the only unexplored thing she could think of. "Will you be able to afford her? Won't you have to get a job that pays enough to be able to pay for child care, too? What will her life be like with you?"

He stared at her for a long moment, then

began to smile. "You know, the funny thing is, if this had happened a couple of years ago, I wouldn't even consider challenging you for her. And the money, just what you brought up, would have been the major factor."

"Really? What's changed?"

He shrugged. "My father died. My crazy father who made me grow up in a mountain cabin with no running water so I would be close to the earth." He shook his head, bemused. "Once he was gone, I found out he left me the royalties on a patent he'd taken out on an invention of his. It was a way to use a specially developed pulley for lifting extremely heavy loads." He shook his head again, almost laughing. "Go figure. Who knew he was a secret genius? It made a small fortune. And now that fortune is mine."

Her heart fell. He could counter every attack and push her back so easily. "Interesting," she said sadly. "So you're saying you can afford to fight for something you really want."

"Exactly."

She took a deep, trembling breath and fought back tears. "You've got me beat there. I don't have any nice special pile of money."

"Sara…" He reached out and touched her cheek. "I'm sorry. What can I say?"

She shook her head, biting her lower lip and about to retreat. And then her sister, who had obviously been eavesdropping, came into the room like a chill wind.

"Okay, now I've had it," she said, standing before them both with her hands on her hips. "The two of you need to get beyond this stuff. The train is coming down the track. The whistle is blowing and the light is coming around the bend. There's no more time for nonsense. It's obvious what you need to do. Get real."

They both stared at her in surprise and she glared right back.

"You've both got great claims to this beautiful child—pending the DNA results, of course. But it looks pretty clear that you both deserve her. There's only one real solution." She shrugged dramatically.

"I'll tell you what I think. This is it. This will answer all your problems and make everyone happy. You've got to do it."

She paused for full effect, then threw out her arms. "You've got to get married."

It was as though an electric explosion

had gone off in the room, almost flattening them both.

"What?" Jake cried out.

"Married!" Sara jumped up, shocked. "What are you talking about?" Her mind reeled.

"Oh, no," Jake was saying, shaking his head emphatically and brushing the whole concept off with his hand. "I don't do 'married.'"

"Maybe you didn't do 'married' in the past," Jill said, looking very stern. "But things have changed. You're not just thinking for yourself now. What Savannah needs is more important than what you may think you need. She needs a mom and a dad. Just like every child. Are you going to deny her that?"

Sara was shaking her head. "Jill, be serious. We're not getting married."

Jill held up a hand to her sister. It was Jake she was aiming at. "Do you have somebody else you want to marry?" she demanded of him.

"No!" He looked as though he was about to start tearing his hair out. "Don't you get it? I never wanted to get married. I never plan to. I'm not going to be tied down to a relationship with someone I might…" His voice faded and he flushed, not sure what he'd been about to say, but sure it really had nothing to do with Sara. Maybe he ought to just shut up for a while.

"Change your thinking, bud," Jill snapped at him. "Stop being so selfish. You've got to think for two."

Sara watched the scene, too stunned to say anything. Where on earth had this idea come from? Had Jill noticed how she was beginning to respond to Jake in a wholly inappropriate way? Was that behind all this talk?

It was a strange sort of love and hate blend that she felt for the man. That didn't do well in a marriage, she wouldn't think. But what did she know? She'd never been married before and Jill was on her second try.

She shook her head, trying to clear her mind. "Jill," she said, her voice choked with emotion. "Go. Please just go."

Her sister watched her uncertainly for a moment, then nodded. "Okay. But don't forget what I've said. Take it seriously."

"Go."

"Okay. Bye." And she left the room.

Jake rose and took Sara's hands in his. He

looked at her with sadness and compassion in his eyes, but she could see that he was immovable.

"I am truly sorry, Sara," he said softly. "But it's a no go. She's my child. I need to be the one who takes care of her."

Sara nodded. For a moment, she couldn't speak. "Where will you go?" she asked when she could manage to control her voice.

"I don't know yet. I'll have to figure out where will be best for us."

She nodded, staring at the top button on his shirt. "Will you let me come see her?"

He squeezed her hands. "Of course."

She looked up into his eyes. Her own were swimming in tears. Was there anything left to say?

"I've got to go," he told her. "I've got some... meetings planned. I'm already late."

She looked at the clock. She was torn. A part of her wanted him gone so that she could go to her room and cry until she had it back under control. Another part just wanted him to stay. "It's almost dinnertime."

He gave her a crooked grin. "I ate enough

at the party to last me for three days. I really need to go. I've got to prepare for tomorrow."

Her heart sank. She knew exactly what he meant.

"Okay. You'll be back tomorrow."

"Of course."

For just a moment, she thought he was going to bend down and kiss her. But he hesitated and then dropped her hands and turned away. "Goodbye," he said at the door, turning back to nod at her. "And, Sara, I really am sorry."

She watched him go and then she cried.

Hours later, she was still in agony but her tears were dry. She helped her sister prepare a light dinner, though she couldn't eat a thing. She played with Savannah, but her heart was pounding and her mind was reeling. She couldn't relax and she couldn't stop thinking about finding ways to keep her baby.

Jill could sense the turmoil she was in and was afraid she would have a stroke.

"Will you stop pacing and sit down? Take a bath. Watch a movie. Calm down. You're going to end up in the hospital."

Sara shook her head. "I can't stop thinking. I have to find a way to convince him...."

"You won't." Jill winced at her own words, knowing they were hurtful. "Oh, Sara, you won't. His mind is made up."

She stared at her sister as though she just didn't understand. "I have to."

Jill looked to Connor, appealing for help, but he shrugged and went out to the garage. She turned back to Sara.

"Well, think about it from his side..." she began.

"I don't want to think about it from his side!" Sara cried. "I just care about my side right now. Savannah's side. The important side." She shook her head in despair. "Jill, my side is to protect this baby. I have to keep her near me. I have to."

"Sara, six months ago we had to talk you into taking her. You didn't want to adopt. You didn't think you could handle a baby in your life."

Sara met her sister's gaze with a bit of defiance in her own. "Six months ago I was a different person."

"I know. You're right." Jill threw her arms

around Sara and hugged her. "It was such a brave thing to do. And you are so good with her. You gave up everything to take her and it has worked out so beautifully."

Sara closed her eyes. "Until Jake showed up."

"Yes." Jill released her, watching her carefully. "But you know, it's possible…life can go on…."

"Really?" Sara turned on her sister fiercely. "You really think my life can go on without my baby?" She started off toward her room. "Then you don't know me as well as you think you do."

CHAPTER EIGHT

THE AGENCY CALLED to tell Sara that the DNA test results were in. The caller couldn't tell her what they were. Someone would be calling about nine the next morning to go over them with her. They just wanted to check that she would be there to receive the call when it came, and she promised she would.

She hung up trembling and looked at the clock. In fifteen hours her fate would be sealed. She had to talk to Jake. Had they called him, too? Or only her? And what would that mean?

She called his number. It rang and rang, and she'd almost given up, when a woman answered.

"Hello," she said smoothly. "Jake Martin's residence."

Sara nearly choked with outrage. He had a

woman over while she was going through all this alone?

"Where's Jake?" she ground out hoarsely.

"Uh… He's taking a shower right now. May I take a message?"

So on top of everything else, he was going to have his women hanging around. Impossible! That was no way to try to raise a little girl.

"Tell him Sara is coming over," she said. To heck with their plans. "I'll be there in half an hour."

She freshened up, grabbed a jacket and started the walk down the hill, on her way over to the house next to her own. It took about five minutes. There was no strange car in the driveway, but that didn't necessarily mean anything. She went to the door and rang.

Jake opened the door and smiled at her. His hair was still wet from his shower and he wore a nice snug T-shirt and clean, but torn and faded jeans. He stood back and motioned for her to enter. She came in but she looked around suspiciously.

"Where is she?" she demanded.

Jake looked around, too, as though totally at sea. "Who?"

"That woman you had here."

He pretended to frown but his eyes were sparkling. "What woman?"

Her frown was real. "She answered the phone when I called."

His face cleared. "Oh. That woman."

"Yes."

"Her name is…let's see." He glanced down at a paper on the counter. "Patty Boudine." He tapped the paper and looked pleased with himself. "That's the one."

Sara frowned, knowing he was teasing her. "So where is she?"

"She's gone." He grinned again. "Sara, I was interviewing her for a job."

That stopped her short. "Really?"

"Yes, really." He mocked her tone. "I put out an ad for a nanny. She showed up. End of story."

She frowned again. "She said you were taking a shower."

"I was. I had to get rid of all that birthday party stickiness I ended up sporting," he said. "I left her out here filling out the application.

Then I asked her a few questions, and she left." He shrugged. "Hey, I thought you would approve. You know I need help." Then he got an idea. "Maybe you should help me choose the nanny. You're the expert, after all. You know what I should be looking for."

He was acting as though it was all a done deal. Her heart was so broken. "You can't even wait a few weeks to see how this takes before you set up a whole support structure around this?"

He saw her despair and he reached for her, taking her by the shoulders and gently holding her in front of him. "Sara sweet Sara, how many ways do I have to tell you? I'm taking my baby with me. Even if it breaks your heart."

She nodded, holding back tears. "It does."

"I know."

She looked at him and everything in her wanted to melt into his arms and let him protect her—but at the same time, he was the one she had to be protected from. It made no sense. But emotions seldom did. She pulled away before she found herself letting temptation rule.

"Are your friends gone?" she asked, walking to the kitchen and peeking in, just to make sure he'd had the damage from the other day cleaned up. And he had. The room sparkled like new.

"They're gone for now. But they could show up again at any moment."

She turned to look at him. "Do they come over every night?" What a nightmare. First these huge, rough men would be hanging around. And then, the women. Despite the one she'd talked to on the phone turning out to be a job applicant, she was pretty sure other women would be showing up. It just fit the scenario. Savannah didn't belong here!

"Pretty much." Suddenly he seemed uncomfortable. "They're trying to talk me into something. I'm resisting for now." His smile was less casual. "They're working on me just like you're working on me. Everybody wants a piece of me. Maybe everybody ought to just leave me alone."

She looked at him speculatively. She wanted to talk to him, but she didn't want to be interrupted by his friends.

"Walk with me," she suggested. It would

soon get dark, but the forecast called for a full moon rising and there ought to be enough light for quite some time. "Let's walk on the beach. Out to the point."

He shrugged. "Why not?"

And a few minutes later, they started off. The light was fading leaving the ocean a gorgeous midnight-blue. The regular beat of the waves on the sand seemed to echo their steps. A cool ocean breeze caught her hair and sent it out behind her like a banner. She lifted her face to it, breathing it in.

"Did they call you?" she asked him at last.

"Who?"

"The agency."

"Yes, they did." He turned to look at her. "I told them I'd be with you tomorrow for the call."

She nodded. That was what she'd thought he would want to do. "You don't plan to take her, though," she said, suddenly scared she might have misjudged him. "I mean even if they…"

"No," he said quickly. "Don't worry. All in good time." He shrugged. "I don't have all my ducks in a row yet. I need to make preparations."

Relief surged through her. She needed more time and so did he.

He stopped and gazed down at her, his face set and earnest. "I think you know what the verdict is going to be, though. I'm Savannah's father. There's no doubt."

She took a deep breath and summoned up all her courage.

"I am going to have to accept that, if the data comes in favoring you," she said, her voice a bit shaky. "And I can accept that legally, you have full rights to her, if that does happen." She looked hard into his eyes and said the hard part. "But regardless, I think you should let me keep her."

He made a face, as though he couldn't believe she'd said that.

"Sara…"

"I'm serious. Think about it. I'm a single woman. But you're a single man. You don't have a clue how to handle this. I'm ready. I've learned a lot. And we've bonded, she and I, big time."

He stared at her for a long moment, and

then he began to walk again and she hurried to catch up with him.

"She's my baby, Jake," she said a bit breathlessly, having a hard time with the sand. "She's been mine for six months. If you take her away, it will be wrenching for her. You don't want to do that kind of damage to a child."

He kept walking. She noticed that his hands were clenched into fists at his side. He was angry, but she'd expected that. This was a gut-wrenching thing they were discussing. Of course he was emotional. So was she.

"I want her," he said at last, his voice a harsh growl of a sound. "More than anything in the world. I want my baby."

Her heart sank. He really meant it. There was no give in his tone, no hint of even the possibility of compromise. She was going to have to go further and think things through a bit more.

"I understand that," she said quickly. "You see, I think I can work out a plan where I can keep her but you won't have to totally give her up."

His grunt signaled disdain, but she didn't waver.

"Hear me out, Jake. You owe me that much."

He stopped and turned to glare down at her.

"Is it because of what happened this afternoon with the mint drops?" he asked. "Are you afraid I'm going to hurt her?"

She was surprised. Funny, but that was the furthest thing from her mind right now.

"I know you would never hurt her." She touched him, put a hand flat against his chest, just above the heart. There was only a thin sheet of cotton between her hand and a hard sense of pounding that spoke of life and determination. It almost scared her to feel it.

"I overreacted. I shouldn't have yelled at you like that." She tried to smile at him. "And you were the one who saved her."

He stared at her and placed his hand over hers, trapping it against his flesh. "So what's your plan?" he asked softly.

She took a deep breath, trying to focus. It was hard when he was so close, so warm.

"Listen, Jake," she said at last. "We could work something out. If…if you just leave her with me, you could go on with your life and not have to give up everything. I would have her here and you could come and go. She would always be here for you and..."

He was frowning. She knew without being told that he didn't like the idea. "It all sounds very nice but it just won't work. What if you get married?"

She brushed that away. "Oh, don't worry about that. I won't. I don't even want to— ever."

He grimaced and shook his head. "You say that now, but there will come a time..."

"No!"

He cupped her cheek with his free hand and gazed down into her eyes. "Sara, you're still so young. You need a man in your life. You know it. You're going to begin longing for it. You'll fall in love."

"No," she said, but this time it almost sounded like a whimper.

His mouth turned up at the corners, but his eyes didn't warm. "Yes. Deep down, you know it's true." His hand caressed the side of her face. "You feel a tug toward me right now. You want human contact. You want me to kiss you."

She was breathless now, and all she could do was shake her head. Her heart was beating like a bird in a cage.

"Don't try to deny it," he said so softly she could hardly hear his voice over the sound of the waves. "I'm going to prove it to you."

His mouth took hers with ease. She didn't put up much of a fight. Because he was right. She wanted his kiss. She'd been wanting it from the day she met him.

The contrast between the cool air and his hot mouth was the first thing that stunned her. And then there was his taste, like buttered honey in the sun, like a sip of red wine in the moonlight, like liquid gold, all wrapped into a racy sensation that sent her senses reeling.

She clung to him, her arms reaching up under his jacket to get as close to his heat as she could. His tongue rasped against hers in a gesture that made her moan low in her throat. His hands slid down to take control of her hips and pull them in hard against his and she welcomed it, pushing against him and hearing small whispered noises of pleasure coming from her own mouth.

She wanted him. Every part of her wanted

him, every part of her was on fire. She was almost drowning in desire. She, who had always been so cool and collected, a reserved observer instead of a committed partner in affairs of the heart and soul, suddenly wanted this man with a sense of pure animal hunger that scared her witless.

Her mind finally fought its way back to the surface and she began to realize what she was doing. She cried out in anguish and pushed away from him, panting as she stared at him, hating him and adoring him at the same time.

"That wasn't fair," she managed to mutter at him, wiping her mouth with the back of her hand. "That was pure ambush. I wasn't ready to defend myself."

His grin was bittersweet and he tried to hide it. "Sara, my beautiful Sara," he said, shaking his head. "You've got something smoldering inside that's just waiting to break out into a forest fire. You can't hold it back forever. Someday, you won't be able to stop. You won't even want to. I think you just proved my point for me."

She glared at him. "You cheated," she said. "I'm not usually like that. And I won't be again. I can control myself. It won't happen again."

He shook his head. "We're talking years and years. You'll meet someone. The spark will light the flame. You'll want to marry him. And you'll have my child living with you." He shrugged. "How would we work that out?"

"No, I swear that will never happen."

He gazed down at her as though she were a recalcitrant child. "You can swear all you want. Life does things to us that we never expect. Happens all the time."

She knew he was right, but that didn't give her a tidy argument for her plans and ideas. She turned away and began walking toward the point as fast as she could go.

Once she'd reached the end of the spit of land, she found a rock and sat on it, looking out at the black ocean. It was dark now, and the mood was somber. Jake came up and sat on the rock next to hers. They stared out to sea, watching a boat in the distance, its lights shimmering over the dark waters.

"Tell me more about Kelly," she said, looking at him in the moonlight. "Tell me what she was like."

He frowned, concentrating on it, trying to wake up his memory. "You know, so many things happened to me right after I knew her, I have to admit, she doesn't stand out like she should. I mean, within a month I was back in the jungle, flirting with daily danger. And then I got caught and spent a lot of time being starved and tortured and trying to figure out how to escape. I wasn't mulling over my relationship with Kelly, if you know what I mean."

"Okay. You've made it clear that you two weren't exactly the love story of the century. And that's too bad, because we need a backstory on all that. We need to remember her better than we do now."

He frowned, shaking his head. "Why? What's the point?"

She turned to look at him. "There will come a day, not too far away, when Savannah will come to you—or come to me—and ask about her mother. And we need to be ready for that."

He stared at her, struck by the thought of it. "Oh, jeez. You're right."

She nodded. "So we ought to put together what memories we have right now, before they slip away, and be prepared to give her a bright, loving picture of the woman who is her true biological mother. Someday, she'll want to know."

He looked out at the ocean again and thought about it. "You know, I think I can remember a lot more than I was dredging up before. Kelly was fun and full of life. I'll work on it. I'll get some anecdotes together and we can go over them."

Sara stretched, feeling suddenly happier. "Great. I'll get Jill to help. I know we can come up with a great character sketch. We'll be ready for her when the time comes."

She smiled at him, but her smile faded quickly. After all, she was taking a lot for granted. What made her think that she would still be around Savannah when those questions began to pop up? Still, she could do her best to help. Savannah was the one who would benefit, no matter who gave her the picture she needed of her birth mother.

The trip back to Jill's house seemed to go by much faster than the trip out to the point had. They arrived in the front yard and Sara turned to face him again, wishing she could think of something to say, some way to cap off this day, that would change his mind and make him see how much better things would be if he left Savannah with her.

"Tomorrow will change everything," he said, almost as though he was warning her.

"Maybe." She searched his face, the lines around his mouth, and she remembered the kiss they'd shared. She could feel herself blushing, even though he probably couldn't see it in the dark.

But he was moving closer, moving with firm deliberation. He wrapped his hand in her hair, winding it slowly, then using it to pull her up close.

"Oh, no," she whispered, melting against him. "Not again. What are you doing?"

"Kissing you." His lips touched hers softly, then again. The feeling was completely different than it had been before. There was no fire behind his gestures, no sense of danger. Every move he made, every way he touched her, was filled with gentle affection. She felt as though she was floating on a cloud.

"No," she said, but there wasn't much force behind it. She was already under his spell.

"Yes." He tipped her chin up so that she had to look into his eyes. "I'm kissing you, Sara, because I need to. I need to hold you. I need to let you know how I feel in ways I can't put in words. Can you understand that?"

She was losing herself in his somber blue eyes. "Maybe," she admitted.

"I'm kissing you because I'm going to break your heart and the way I feel about you now, I can hardly stand the thought of it."

"Then don't do it," she murmured.

"I have no choice. And it's going to kill me." He groaned, rocking her in his arms. "Sara, I like you. You're adorable. You've been so good for Savannah. And I'm going to hurt you so badly. I hate doing it. But there is no other way."

She sighed. She was already hurt beyond tears. "I should go in," she said.

"Yes." He released her and watched as she went to the door. "Good night," he whispered.

Turning, she wanted to kiss him again. Soaking in everything she was beginning to love about him, his thick, tousled hair, his handsome face, his strong, solid body, she took a step in his direction. Then she stopped, trying to read the look on his face, wondering…

No. Disappointment flooded her heart, and then chagrin. His eyes were hooded, his face could have been chiseled from stone. She couldn't do that. She couldn't let herself run back into his arms. Enough.

"Good night," she said, and she went inside and closed the door.

Jake awoke with a start. He glanced at the clock. It wasn't six yet. There was someone in his house.

He rolled out of bed silently, picked up a knife and made his way toward the living room. A shadowy figure was coming through from the kitchen. He pressed himself against the wall and waited.

He could see that it was a woman. He half wanted it to be Sara, but he didn't think it was. He waited. As she came closer, he tensed, and as she came even with where he was standing, he lunged forward and grabbed her, holding the knife to her throat.

She screamed.

"Who are you?" he rasped with his mouth against her ear.

"Jake! It's Jill. Cut it out."

He knew right away she was telling the truth, and he relaxed, letting her go and putting down the knife. Then he stared at her, shaking his head.

"What the hell are you doing?" he demanded. "I could have hurt you badly. You can't come in like that. Don't you know how to knock?"

She laughed, coming into full focus as he turned on a light. "Sorry. I'm really good friends with the people who own this house and I know where the extra key is hidden. I had to come in before this crazy day gets started and talk to you for a minute."

He shook his head. "You want me to make some coffee?" he growled.

"No. Thanks anyway."

He folded his arms across his chest and nodded. "Okay. Talk."

"I'm not going to make a long speech out of this," she began.

"Good," he muttered, making a face.

She hesitated, then added, "And I'm not very good at talking people into things."

"Good again," he said softly.

"But I need to say my piece. I need you to know how this looks to me. Jake, you know that you will probably be declared Savannah's father today. That means you have a completely new responsibility to that adorable child. It's going to be up to you to make sure she gets the launch into life she deserves. You need the best advice and the best help you can find. And I know how you can get it."

He looked at her coolly and waited for her to finish. He had a feeling he already knew where this was going. And sure enough, it went right where he thought it would. After all, Jill had tipped her hand before and she seemed to be like a bulldog with a very tasty bone.

"You and Sara need to get married," she declared, making it sound like a judgment from on high.

He groaned. "Sara and I barely know each other."

"So what? You'll grow together. Some of the best marriages in history started out that way. That means nothing in the long run. Lots of people who think they are madly in love then find out differently once they get married. I think you know that."

"I know it, and I don't care. I don't want to get married. I never wanted that. And I never will."

"Your baby needs a mother."

He groaned again. "Jill…"

"You know it's true. And if you won't provide one for her, you're going to regret it someday."

He shrugged. "So be it."

Her shoulders drooped. "Jake, don't be that way. Think about it. You can both help each other and in the process, you'll be making life a lot better for your child. That is the best recipe for a good marriage. Mutual benefit. One of those marriage of convenience things."

He was shaking his head. "What makes you think that growing to love each other thing will work?"

"I know you both. You're good people, with good hearts. You both love someone better than you love yourselves." She was close to tears now. She was obviously completely invested in this emotionally. "It'll work. Believe me. You're fated to join together. It's written in the stars."

He stared at her for a long moment, then shook his head. "Okay, Jill. You said your piece. I understand your point of view. You can go now."

She nodded with a sigh. "I'm done. But I had to do it." She started for the door, then looked back. "Are you coming over for the call?"

"Yes."

"Good. See you then."

He closed his eyes and leaned against the wall, waiting to hear her car leave. Had her diatribe done any good in clearing up the way for him to do what he had to do? Not at all. He felt horrible about ripping Savannah away from Sara, but he didn't see any way around it. It had to be done.

Good. She was gone. He turned back toward his bedroom, but something stopped him. Had she come back? He looked out onto the driveway and saw one of his friends pulling up. He sighed.

"Doesn't anybody respect morning sleep

anymore?" he muttered, and got ready for company. This one would want coffee. He was sure of it.

Sara heard the sound of knuckles knocking softly on the front door. She glanced at the clock. It wasn't even eight yet. He was early.

She went to let him in, opening the door and making a face as she saw him. It had been a long, sleepless night and she knew she looked terrible. She was pretty sure the startled expression on his face as he saw her gave evidence to that fact.

"Come on in," she said. "I do look like death warmed over and I know it."

He gave her a strange smile and said, "You look beautiful to me."

Something cloudy was swirling in his gaze and she couldn't get a read on what it was. Was he feeling awkward because of what happened the night before? No, she couldn't believe that.

She didn't feel awkward. She'd gone over it and over it in her mind, all night long, and she'd decided that she knew what had happened and why. She'd fallen in love with Jake.

The trouble was, he didn't love her. And that made all the difference.

"Would you like some Bundt cake?" she asked. "We've got plenty."

"I'd love some," he answered. "Give me a giant piece. I need sustenance for a day like this."

"For the phone call?"

"That," he agreed, "and so much more."

She squinted at him curiously, but his smile was enigmatic, and she turned to get him coffee and a slice of Chocolate Decadence instead of pushing the issue. She put his delicious breakfast in front of him, handed him a fork and stood back leaning on the opposite chair, watching him.

He was so beautiful; the most handsome man she'd ever known. Just looking at his square-jawed face and his gorgeously muscular body made her want to go ahead and swoon. Did he know how she felt about him? He had to know she was smitten, but he didn't have a clue about how deep the feelings went. She hadn't known until last night, but now she was sure of it.

Or was she just kidding herself? She'd only

known him for a few days. Was that enough for falling in love? Of course not. It was just silly to think she knew enough about him to fall all the way.

Still, it had been a pretty intense few days they'd known each other. They'd done a lot of living, faced a lot of heartbreak, found a sort of comfort with each other that she'd never known before, all in that short time. And time was short. She probably wasn't going to be seeing him for much longer. She might as well live for love while she could.

Should she tell him how she felt? No. He would just pull back if she did. She couldn't risk that. But she did have one last play she was going to make, one last idea of how they could both keep Savannah in their lives. She wasn't hopeful, but she was determined.

"Have you got something new and interesting on your mind?" she asked, because it occurred to her that he appeared as though he did. There was definitely an idea brewing inside him. But he just smiled and said, "Let me eat first."

She slipped down into the chair and leaned

forward, watching him. "So there is something new."

He swallowed a bite of cake and made a face indicating ecstasy. "Your sister is a fantastic baker lady," he mentioned in passing.

"That's not news," she said crisply.

"I realize that." He smiled at her. "Give me a few more minutes, okay? I do have something to talk to you about. I've had a couple of visitors this morning and I've done a lot of thinking. As a result, I've got a new perspective on some things. Tell you about it in a minute."

"Okay," she said, squirming impatiently in her chair. "And then I have something I want to tell you."

"What is it?"

"It's one last idea I've got for a solution to our problem. I've had some new thinking as well. I just want to run it past you and then let you think about it, too."

He shrugged. "Go for it."

She shook her head. "I want to hear your news first."

He smiled and reached out to take her hand in his. "Okay, I guess it's time to tell you."

"I'm ready," she said, smiling back and marveling at this new affectionate look in his eyes when he spoke to her. She loved it.

Bringing her hand to his lips, he dropped a kiss in her palm, then released her so he could push away his empty plate. Sitting back in his chair, he grew serious.

"Okay, I'm going to tell you about my childhood and what I learned by growing up in some pretty tough circumstances." He looked at her. "I want you to know about it and how it makes me what I am today."

She nodded. "Okay."

He looked into the distance. "Sara, I was raised by a single father. My mother died when I was very young. I didn't have the advantage of a woman to nurture me. All I had was a mean, grouchy father who expected me to be a man at twelve. I know how much I lost because of that."

He drew back to look into her face again.

"I grew up in a house where a grunt meant 'good morning' and a glare meant, 'isn't it time you got the hell out of here and left me alone?' That was pretty much the extent of our communications when I was young. When it came to family, all I knew was what I saw at the movies."

"Oh, Jake!" She reached out to take his hand in hers and he leaned closer to her.

"I've always thought that my inability to fall in love, to really feel close to women I spent time with, was because my emotions were stunted by the way I was raised. I didn't know how to love. I didn't have that imprinting growing up. I was more like a wolf cub, just managing to survive in the woods. I thought I'd never get married, never have children."

Her fingers tightened on his hand. Her heart ached for that young boy, growing up wild.

"And then, a miracle happened. And there was Savannah." He shook his head, looking bemused, as though he still couldn't believe it. "My whole world changed. My first reaction was—this is ridiculous. I can't take care of a baby. I've never been around one before. I would have to give up my whole way of life."

He smiled at her.

"But then I looked at the pictures Kelly had sent me, and I began to fall in love. And I began to realize having that baby would connect me to humanity in a way I'd never been connected before. She would be my lifeline. She would be my life."

His fingers curled around hers and held her tight.

"I'm not giving up Savannah. I think you understand that by now. She's mine and she's a part of me."

He blinked hard and she realized he was more emotional than she'd thought. His story of his childhood had touched her deeply. She knew he was right—she understood. He wasn't going to give his baby up, not for anything. She knew exactly how he felt.

She looked at him, hesitating and wondering how to approach this. As far as she could see, there was only one hope left. Reaching out, she took both his hands in hers and gazed at him with tears in her own eyes.

"I know, Jake," she said softly. "Believe me, I understand."

He cleared his throat and coughed, obviously not ready to go on, and she assumed he was finished.

"Jake, I know you can't give her up and I can't really ask you to. But I told you I had one last lone crazy idea to help solve our problem. Last night you were interviewing for a nanny to help you with her. You're obviously going to need somebody."

She shrugged and smiled at him.

"I want that job. Please." She held on to his hands tightly. "Please let me stay with her. I'll be quiet and discrete and won't…"

"No."

"No?" Her broken heart fell into pieces before him. "No?" It was a cry from her soul. "But, Jake…"

He tugged on her hands and pulled her up to face him as he rose. "No. Because, Sara, I've been thinking it over. And I think Jill is right. I think we ought to get married."

"You think…what?" Stunned, she could only stare at him, not sure she understood.

He stared down at her earnestly.

"I don't want my baby growing up without a mother like I did. I know from personal experience how important it is to have a mother behind you, to keep you strong and make you understand what is right and what is wrong. To give you love and teach you compassion for other living things. To teach you how to dream." He shook his head, about to get too emotional again. "She needs a father for a lot of things, but a mother is indispensible. Gotta have one."

He searched her eyes, gauging how she felt about it, but her mouth was wide-open and she was staring at him as though he'd suddenly turned green.

He touched her cheek. "I know you said you were dead set against getting married. But I know if you think it over and…"

"I said what?" she demanded, finally getting her voice. "Oh, no. That was then. This is now. I…I've been rethinking a lot of stupid opinions I once had."

A sudden grin broke on his face. "Sara…"

"See? I can change my mind, too."

"All the better."

"But, Jake, are you…? Do you really mean…?"

"I'm asking you to marry me, Sara. Please say yes."

CHAPTER NINE

IT WAS ALMOST nine o'clock and they didn't have much time for celebration, but they celebrated anyway. Jill came downstairs, carrying Savannah, who cried out with joy when she caught sight of Jake, spreading her arms to be taken up by him.

He took her and began to dance around the room, then grabbed Sara to join them. They were laughing and crying and explaining things to Jill, and then to Connor when he came into the room, when the phone rang.

The seriousness of the morning came surging back. Sara took one receiver and put it on speaker, while Jake took another, just in case. Mrs. Truesdale, the counselor on the line was the one they had each spoken to previously, and she launched right into it. Her explanation was filled with percentages and probabilities and all kinds of technical and scientific terms for the raw data in the results, most of it going right over Sara's head. She was too filled with happiness and wonder at Jake's proposal to have room in her heart or her mind to try to analyze things she only barely understood. But the gist of it all was pretty much what they had expected. Jake had been proven to be Savannah's biological father. It was all over on that score.

Mrs. Truesdale advised them to take a look at some forms she had sent them by email. She'd also posted the full document for them to look over and she advised them to take note of the final paragraph which described the grace period and what it meant.

"Here's what that is all about," she said. "There will be a grace period during which the father will take possession of the baby, but finalization won't be complete for three months. During this period, the previous guardian has the right to file an appeal. She might want to consult an attorney as to how she might do that and under what terms. It would be best if both of you were to familiarize yourselves with the rules and guidelines of our conditions so that you can judge whether the new guardian's activities and attitudes are in line with agency recommendations. I've emailed you that information."

"So I'm on probation?" Jake asked, a little startled by the news.

Sara frowned. She hadn't realized it but she had gone through the same trial period. Apparently she'd passed with flying colors. She made a mental note to check it out so that she could make sure Jake didn't do anything that might cause any problems.

For some reason, they didn't tell the counselor about their marriage plans. Maybe because they were so new—maybe for some other reason. Who knew?

They did hear about papers that had to be signed and agreed to meet Mrs. Truesdale in Seattle within the week to do so. And then hung up and looked at each other with shining eyes and got back to celebrating.

Sara spent the next few days in a blur of happiness, interrupted periodically by moments of panic when she wondered if all this was really true. Could she be dreaming? Making it up in her own demented mind that might be trying to compensate for the horror she'd been contemplating if she lost her baby? It was all just too good to be true.

But then Jake would come by and the two of them would play with Savannah and take her on a picnic or a ride across the bay to a forest or a fun zone and she would know that this was what life was going to be like from now on. She couldn't imagine anything better.

There were other moments when she wondered if Jake was having second thoughts about it all. He was aloof at times, staring off into the distance, thinking hard about something he didn't seem to want to share with her. She wondered if he regretted what he'd done.

But there wasn't much time to worry about that. There was a wedding to plan!

Jill was in heaven. Sara had done most of the heavy duty planning on her wedding to Connor just months before, and now she was going to be able to pay her back with her own hard work.

Sara spent most of her time moving things back into her beach house. The workmen had finished and everything was gorgeous, but new furniture was a must—especially for the nursery.

At the same time, she could pop in and say "hi" to Jake next door any time she felt like it. And that was a lot. She got to know his friends better by being so close, and that was a good thing. They were all, without exception, remarkable men once she got to know the personalities behind the tough guys images. They all seemed to have nicknames, like Mr. Danger, or Two Speed. Jake was called Cool Hand and his best friend was a tall, handsome guy named Starman.

Sara asked him about how he got his nickname one day when he was helping her fold the sheets she'd just washed and dried.

"So why do they call you Starman?" she asked him.

He looked puzzled at her question. "Why not?"

She shrugged. "Does that mean you're interested in the stars? Or did you want to be an astronaut when you were younger?" She looked at him curiously.

"No." He frowned as though he was beginning to think she might have a screw loose.

"They call me Starman because it's my last name. Kevin Starman."

"Oh." She laughed, chagrined. "I hadn't thought of that one."

He was a gentle giant, but she had a feeling she might not recognize the man he turned into in a firefight.

Jill was so busy preparing for the wedding, she hardly saw her long enough to say more than two words to until the day before the ceremony was scheduled.

"This has all been happening so fast," Jill said, looking at her sister searchingly. "We haven't had any time to talk." She frowned. "Are you sure about this?"

Sara's smile was glowing. "Are you kidding? It's saving my life."

"Yes, but…" She made a face of concern.

"Don't worry." She patted Jill's hand. "We get along great, and we both love Savannah. Everything will be fine."

Jill shook her head. "I don't know. I hate to think I helped push you into something like this. I mean—you should be marrying someone you love. Someone you can build a life with…"

She waved that away. "Savannah *is* my life. This will help her. That's all I care about."

"But, you'll be tied to Jake and…"

She hugged her sister. "Jill, don't worry. I haven't even thought twice about that. Seriously. No second thoughts at all. I'm ready. I want to do this."

She hesitated, wondering if she should tell her sister the truth. No, she would just worry even more if she knew—that Sara was head over heels in love with Jake. No doubt about it. No other man in the world would ever cause her to waver. She loved him.

It was a strange place to be in, something she'd thought would never happen to her. But it had, and right in time, too. The trouble was, she had no idea how he felt about her and it terrified her to make guesses. What was he thinking?

"You don't really know him, you know," Jill said, giving her a start. Was Jill reading her mind?

"Jill, aren't you the one who went cruising over to his house before dawn and set this whole marriage thing up?"

"Yes, but…" Jill frowned thoughtfully.

"When you come right down to it, I don't really think I was the one who talked him into it."

Sara stared at her. "What are you talking about?"

"Oh, I tried all right. I tried very hard, because you were so miserable and I couldn't stand seeing you that way. But when I left him that morning, he was still totally unconvinced. At least, that was the way he seemed to me."

Sara shrugged. "Then what do you think sent him over the edge?" she asked.

Jill thought for a moment. "You know what? I think it was his friend, that Starman fellow. I saw him pulling up just as I was leaving the house that morning. I'd done all I could and I thought I'd failed." She shrugged again. "I left in deep depression, thinking all was lost. Two hours later, Jake was at our house asking you to marry him." Her eyes narrowed and she pressed her lips together as she thought about it. "Starman must have said something that convinced him."

Sara frowned as well. That seemed odd. She would ask Jake about it someday. Right now, she didn't want to risk upsetting any apple carts, so she wasn't going to ask questions about anything. Once they were married and it was a done deal, then she would get creative and curious. But until then, she was treading carefully.

But what did it matter? They *were* getting married. Savannah was going to have a mother and a father. Whatever happened between her and Jake as a result—well, that was still to come, and they would deal with it as it happened. For now, she was a happy woman.

The wedding was on the beach in front of Sara's newly renovated house. And, incidentally, in front of the house Jake was renting. Very convenient. The ceremony was small and private. Jake had a small group of friends, mostly Army buddies that Sara had seen hanging out at his house—including Starman as his best man. Jill and Connor brought the twins and took care of Savannah. Luckily they had a family preacher they could contribute to the mix, and he turned out to be wonderful. Sara had invited a few of her friends from the magazine she'd worked for over the years. That was it. A small but elegant family wedding.

It was a beautiful morning. The sun was shining on the ocean and the blue of the water contrasted to the blue of a sky filled with white, puffy clouds. Sara felt like she was walking on air.

Jill had married Connor just months before and she'd loaned Sara her wedding dress. It was white and lacy and quite traditional. The bodice was form-fitting and encrusted with seed pearls, as was the edging on the veil. She carried purple irises and felt like a queen.

Jake had balked, but in the end, he'd agreed to wear a tuxedo. He was looking very handsome. But was he as thrilled as she was? Probably not. Still, she couldn't hold back her joy. She felt like one lucky girl.

Jill had baked the most gorgeous wedding cake she'd ever seen, and after the ceremony, their visitors did their best to eat it all as they stood around and chatted and congratulated the happy couple. She and Jake didn't seem to have any appetite. He kept looking at her and smiling as if they shared some secret joke on everybody else. She couldn't help but laugh. She was so happy.

Starman made a toast to their happiness and she could have sworn he had tears in his eyes. Jill had hired a string quartet who played lovely music during the ceremony and then more modern tunes during the reception, as they ate Jill's cake and laughed a lot. They kicked off their shoes and danced in the sand, with all their friends cheering them on.

A lovely day, simple and elegant. A day to remember, for the rest of their lives.

And then they were alone.

They'd decided to live in Sara's house. It was finished and beautifully decorated—just right to begin a new life in. Jill and Connor had taken Savannah with them for the rest of the day, so that Sara and Jake could settle in and get comfortable before they had to deal with a baby.

They explored the house and she showed off her favorite elements, like the reading nook in the stairway landing, and the glass-enclosed breakfast room that could have served as a greenhouse.

"This is really a nice place," he told her. "I'm beginning to feel downright civilized for the first time in my life."

She smiled at him. "I love this house," she admitted. "And now I'm going to love it even more with you in it."

He turned to look at her, startled, and she flushed, wondering if she'd said too much. There was a frisson of excitement between them. Every nerve she owned seemed to be sizzling. They were married now. What next?

She led the way back downstairs to the kitchen and she began a cheerful line of chatter while she cut them both pieces of their wedding cake and they sat down at her little counter to eat them.

What next?

The question was in the air and in her head. She was talking a mile a minute, but that wasn't helping. What next?

"So this is where we're going to live," he murmured, looking around approvingly. "I've gotta say, I like it. And it seems to be perfect for Savannah."

Sara nodded. "Renovated for her, custom-made." She glanced at him. "What do you foresee doing with your days?" she asked, suddenly wondering why they hadn't explored this topic before. It seemed pretty basic. "Just exactly what are you planning to do?"

He gazed at her levelly. "About what?"

She shrugged. "About earning a living." She'd never imagined that he might plan to just hang around the house. To her, that didn't seem like a proper man's position. Besides, they were going to need the money a job would bring.

"You want me to get a job?" He raised a dark eyebrow and looked at her cynically. "Is that it?"

She lifted her chin, not sure how he was going to react to her answer. "Yes. I think it would be a good thing."

He stared at her for a moment, and she began to get nervous. Then he laughed. "Oh, Sara, you're so conventional."

She smiled in relief. At least he found it funny, not offensive. "Exactly. The old ways are usually the best. Don't you think so?"

He pulled her off her bar stool and into his lap. He held her close and kissed the top of her head.

"Yes. I do think so. And a couple of my buddies and I are planning to start working on a small security firm. We want to emphasize research and development, working on new technology for keeping people safe. I learned to use a lot of technology in the Rangers and I think we can improve on some of the methods and equipment we had available. I'm really excited about our chances."

Well, there it was. Nothing to worry about. He had plans.

"Great. You're planning it for here in Seattle?"

He nodded. "Probably. We may start it out right here in the kitchen and then look for a headquarters in the city once we get going."

"Wow. That's really interesting. I'll help all I can."

He looked at her, considering. "You can work on ad copy when the time comes. You're experienced on that, aren't you?"

She nodded. "I've done PR work and marketing and any kind of writing associated with magazine work. But I meant with start-up money. I've got some saved."

"No." He shook his head. "I would never

ask you to risk your savings for my start-up. Besides, I've got my own stash. My father left me some, remember?"

"Oh, that's right. Good." She grinned at him. "Do a good job and we'll all be Seattle millionaires."

He kissed her neck. "You've got it." Gently he set her down and rose from his stool.

"So, shall we discuss the bed situation?" he said, gazing down at her.

Her breath caught in her throat. Now? Right here? She wasn't ready!

"I think I ought to take the guest bedroom for now," he went on. "What do you think?"

"Oh." Did her disappointment show on her face? She hoped not. "That's very considerate of you."

"This is a marriage of convenience, isn't it?" he asked her softly. "I mean, we didn't marry for love. We married to take care of someone we both love. That's different. Isn't it?"

She felt all the blood drain from her face. "Yes. I suppose so."

"So I think we ought to have separate bedrooms. At least for a while." He shrugged casually and didn't seem all that interested. "I mean, things may change."

"Of course. You're right."

She flushed and turned to hide it. It was for the best, of course. As he said, they hadn't married for love. There was no reason to hurry a physical connection. If he didn't think the time was right, he was probably on the right track. He was obviously much more experienced in these things than she was. She could wait—wait in her cold, lonely bed. Would he ever want to share it with her?

Maybe, someday. As he said, things may change.

But there was a cold, hollow feeling around her heart that night.

Jake had been afraid he would be restless and uneasy with another person living in his house. He didn't mean Savannah, of course. But he did mean Sara. He was used to having a buddy or two flopping in his place at various times, but having a woman who actually lived with him—no, that wasn't in his repertoire of experiences.

To his surprise, he adjusted very quickly. She enjoyed fixing him meals and that came as a sort of gift he hadn't expected. She kept things picked up, which he'd never quite gotten the knack of. And she wasn't one of the chatty types who talked your ear off. She was as quiet as he was most of the time. All in all, he enjoyed having her around.

He watched her feeding Savannah. The joy in her face, Savannah's happy laugh, the sunshine coming in through the breakfast room windows, all contributed to his feeling of happiness and well-being. He didn't deserve to be this happy. He still had promises to keep.

He'd done the right thing—hadn't he? He thought he had. He couldn't have left his child behind, and he needed someone to help take care of her better than he could ever do. So he'd enlisted Sara in the endeavor. Was that fair to her? Maybe not. But so far, it was working out fine.

Still, he wasn't totally sure he'd done the right thing. Was it right to marry Sara, to tie her up in this relationship? Would he have felt as close to any other woman he'd involved in it this way? She seemed so perfect for this role and she shared his joy in Savannah day by day in ways probably no one else could. For now, it seemed all was right with the world.

But there was going to be a big test of that sense of calm coming up soon and he didn't feel he ought to do anything to bring the two of them closer until then. He couldn't completely commit to this relationship until he saw how that came out.

When Sara realized he was going back to the jungle to take care of unfinished business, the truth would be plain for all to see. Could she handle it? Only time would tell.

He had to go. He was going with his mates. There was a job they had to take care of. They'd left too many people behind. The bastards who had treated them so badly had to pay, and they had to make sure that could never happen again in that place. He owed it to his buddies, he owed it to himself. He owed it to the world. That hellhole in the jungle had to be purged.

And once that was done, if he came back alive, they would see where things stood.

Days fell into a pattern of mundane happiness. Sara cared for Savannah, which was her greatest joy, and she took care of Jake, which was getting to be a sweeter task every time she performed some little service for him. She was beginning to understand how doing things for other people could be a precious gift—as long as it was appreciated.

She took Savannah to put her toes in the ocean at least once a day. She took her to the playground. She took her along when she went grocery shopping in the little island market that she loved. She signed up for a "Mommy and Me" swimming class at the local Y and spent time finding just the right outfits to make Savannah the cutest baby on the island. She spent a lot of time cooking up special baby food versions of meals for her child.

But best of all, she shared every minute she could with Jake. No one else in the world could understand how special their baby was. Only Jake. And he joined right in. It was wonderful.

Sharing with Jill and Connor had been fun, but that had nothing on the deep, abiding joy sharing with Jake had for them both. This was what a family ought to feel like. This was as close to heaven as real life could get.

The only problem that nagged at her was the question—how long was Jake going to deny that the two of them should be a total and complete unit as well?

She was afraid there was an answer to that—and not one she was going to like. The truth was out there if she only let herself face it. He didn't love her. And he didn't want to raise her expectation that someday he might.

She had to admit he was generous with kisses, as long as they were simple and affectionate. His hugs were warm and welcoming. But they hadn't had a repeat of the burning encounter they'd had out at the Point that night before he asked her to marry him. Hopes were dimming that real married life was in the cards for them and she wasn't really sure what she could do about it.

So her nights were still empty, though she couldn't really complain. Her days were warm enough to make up for it. And her husband was always there for her in every other way. Maybe that would be enough.

She was getting to know his friends better all the time and she liked them more and more. Starman had a way of showing up just when she needed help to carry in groceries or start the barbecue. She knew Jake felt very close to him.

"I'd say he's my best friend," Jake agreed. "We've been through a lot together. We've saved each other's neck a few times, and we'll probably do it a few times more."

That gave her a chill, but she didn't question it.

One day, about a month after the wedding, she was trying to dig into soil that was hard as a rock in order to prepare for planting a rosebush. Starman showed up and did it for her, giving her a large, perfectly round hole that would leave lots of room for planting mix.

"Thank you so much," she told him. "I was going to ask Jake to dig it for me when he got back from his morning run, but now I won't have to bother him."

Starman put down the shovel and looked at her earnestly. "Sara, I just want to thank you for what you're doing."

"Really?" She smiled at him. "What am I doing?"

"You're really helping us out here. You marrying Jake is going to make all the difference. I know it had to do with the kid and everything, but now he'll be able to relax about that. He's just whacko about that kid."

"Oh, I know. We both are."

"Sure. She's a great kid. But the point is, now that you're someone he can trust to take care of her, he's starting to think straight again. So I just wanted to thank you for that."

He turned to go but she stopped him.

"Wait, Starman. I'm not sure I understand. What was Jake worried about?"

"Who would take care of the kid." He stepped back closer and spoke confidentially. "He was saying he couldn't leave little Savannah alone while we went on missions. But now he's got you to take care of that. He was turning us down, telling us he had new responsibilities and such. We told him we couldn't imagine going without him. And we got him back in gear." He winked at her. "He told me the other day that he'll be coming along." He grinned. "So all is right with the world. Because of you."

He gave her a crisp salute and headed out. She stood staring after him, trying to make sense of what he'd said and very much afraid she understood it only too well.

That night was the first night she heard Jake cry out in the dark. It wasn't a scream exactly.

More of an angry yell. It sounded like swearing, only she couldn't make out the words. When she went in and woke him, he seemed angry about it, and in the morning, he didn't want to talk about what had happened. The whole thing left her more worried than she'd been since the day they'd decided to get married. How could she help him if he wouldn't let her in?

CHAPTER TEN

WAS JAKE PREPARING to go on a mission to Southeast Asia? Was he planning to attack the prison camp where he and his friends were once held? It made Sara sick to think of, but she was afraid he was actually doing exactly that.

What were the chances that he would come back alive? How could he even contemplate doing something so dangerous? Leaving behind Savannah—leaving behind the life they'd begun to build together? It was unthinkable.

She didn't care what the other men did. If they felt they had to go back to the prison camp, maybe to get revenge for the way those guards had hurt them, fine. Let them go. But they didn't have wives and children to think of. Jake did. How could she convince him that this was just wrong?

He'd grown up, as he always said, uncivilized. And this wild sort of living had been his existence for much too long. So maybe he didn't understand that there was a point where a man had to give up the excitement of revenge and fighting.

It was one thing to be a military man, trained and protected by a system. It was another to go off into the jungle with a bunch of guys you palled around with and hope to get the chance to succeed at destroying a prison camp on your own. It was crazy. That much she understood. But did he?

He'd never told her all about what had happened in that Pacific jungle when he was an Army Ranger. She'd seen his naked back up close and personal, studied the scars, even traced one with her finger the day before when they were at the beach and he was lying on his stomach in the sand. Savannah was playing with sand toys and Sara was watching her but paying just as much attention to the man beside her.

"What happened?" she asked him at the time. "Who did this?"

He turned to her. "You don't really want to

know," he said dismissively. "It's not a pretty story." Looking beyond her, he said, "Hey, look at Savannah. She pulled herself up beside the beach chair. That girl is going to take off walking any day now."

Sara swelled with pride for her baby like she always did. "Oh, she's too young for that," she said.

"Are you kidding? Look at her. She wants to run!"

"You should have seen the twins. They were both running at ten months." She laughed. "I was told I was fifteen months before I would trust my legs to carry me. I took my time." She smiled at him. "How about you?"

He shrugged with a sort of studied disinterest. "I didn't have much of a mother. Nobody ever told me stuff like that about my baby days."

Her smile faded and she looked away. "No baby book, huh?" she noted.

He shook his head and she realized he'd turned the conversation away from those scars on his back once again. But now she had to know. It was time he filled her in on the background.

* * *

That night she was determined to get to the bottom of it all.

"All right," she said after the sun had gone down and Savannah had fallen asleep for the night. "Savannah is down, we've had dinner and cleaned up, there's nothing either of us want to watch on TV—it's time for you to open up and tell me a few things I need to know." She pinned him with her steady gaze. "You are going to talk."

"Oh, yeah?" He couldn't help but smile at her, she looked so cute and serious. "What do you want me to talk about?"

"Tell me about what you were doing in the Pacific area for the last couple of years. I know you were an Army Ranger and that you spent some time in a prison camp in the jungle, and I know you've been discharged recently. But what was it you did back then? And why do you have those scars on your back?"

He looked away for a moment, then made a face. "Okay. I guess it is time." He sank down onto the couch and she sat at the other end. "You're right about me being an Army

Ranger. We had a special mission in our unit. We rescued people."

"From what?" she asked in all innocence.

He took a deep breath, searching her face before he told her. "From being kidnapped and tortured by the bad guys."

"Oh." She recoiled. Maybe she really didn't want to know all the details.

"I've been working rescue operations for years. I got pretty damn good at it, too. I rarely got hurt or caught or in any sort of trouble. Until this last time."

"You mean, after you knew Kelly?"

He nodded. "We managed to negotiate a couple of good situations in the Philippines. Then we were sent to a trouble spot in Southeast Asia. A pair of missionaries had been captured by rebels. No one knew where they'd been taken. We spent weeks tracking down their location. We were undercover, pretending to be hippies looking to commune with nature and do drugs."

"What?" She had a hard time seeing him that way.

He threw a half smile her way. "We were pretending, Sara. Trying to blend into the countryside. We made friends with the more primitive people of the area and finally we got a fix on the location we were looking for. It was in the jungle and we executed a beautiful textbook-ready operation. But when we finally got to the site where the missionaries were being held…"

He hesitated, then shrugged and went ahead and told her the truth. "We found nothing but bodies. They were already dead. And left as bait for us." He sighed. "At that point, we were so upset when we saw what had been done to those good people—a man and a woman whose only goal was to help others—we got careless and screwed up and ended up getting captured by the militia of the local strong man who didn't like foreigners coming in. He immediately threw us into his prison camp and tried to get ransom for us."

"Wow." She could hardly breathe. He was sitting here so calmly, telling her things that should only be in movies. No real human beings should have to go through these things. Her heart broke for them all.

"They held us for a few months. They didn't feed us much, but most of the time, they weren't exactly cruel. Just not very nice. But the first time a few of us tried to escape— me and Starman, among them—they caught us and then the really ugly stuff began."

"Is that when you got those scars on your back?" she asked him, wincing as she thought of it.

"Yeah. Starman has the same. They thrashed us the old-fashioned way. They wanted to make sure we didn't do that again."

She shook her head. She didn't want to think about it. It made her sick. "But you did do it again, didn't you?"

He grinned. "Of course we did. That's how stubborn we are. We bided our time and saw another chance and escaped. This time we made it to a city and got help." He moved as though his back was bothering him. "But the punishment lives on," he murmured softly.

"They do look…horrible. Those scars, I mean. I'm surprised you lived through that." She felt nauseous thinking about it.

"I'm kind of surprised, too. And actually, Punky, a friend of ours, didn't. His back got infected and he died."

He said it so simply, as though it was a

common thing. Could have happened to anyone. She had to catch her breath to speak. "I'm so sorry."

"Yeah. Well, that's the breaks. Other guys were there, guys who didn't get away. People we had to leave behind." He grimaced. "They need to be rescued," he said softly.

She bit her lip. She didn't want to hear that.

"See, that's what I have to get you to understand," he said, looking at her with his luminous eyes. "That's what we do. We rescue people."

She stared at him. "But you're not in the service any longer."

He nodded. "I took a discharge. I thought I wanted to move on." He shook his head. "But the faces haunt me, Sara. All those people. They need to be helped. Somebody's got to save them."

Emotion welled in her chest. "Not you."

He turned away and didn't say a word. She moved closer to him on the couch.

"Your friends are planning a trip back there, aren't they?" she said.

He nodded, still looking away.

"Are you going with them?" she asked in a strangled voice.

He winced and ran fingers through his thick hair. "Wow. Listen, I've been meaning to talk to you about that." He looked at her. "I won't be gone long."

Her heart seemed to stop. What was he talking about? He couldn't predict the future. If he went, he might be gone forever. That was impossible. It couldn't happen. She felt a sense of hysteria rising in her throat.

"You know very well you might get killed. Just when Savannah has her father back, you want to take him away again? Are you crazy?"

His face was tortured. "Look, I love Savannah. She's my life. But there are other things in my life, other responsibilities. There's old business that has to be cleared up."

She felt a sense of despair. What could she do to prove to him how wrong this was? "Then take us with you," she demanded.

"What?" He stared at her. "Now you're the one who's sounding crazy."

"We're a family unit. We go where you go. If you need to go so badly, take us with you." She glared at him, daring him to answer.

He shook his head slowly. "You don't have a clue what you're asking. The place where we're going is hell on earth. I wouldn't let you or Savannah within a hundred miles of the place. It can't happen."

"If it's really so bad, you shouldn't go, either!" she cried.

He stared at her, hard. "I have to go. It's my responsibility. I owe too many people to turn back now."

His tone was final and she knew going on with this train of thought was only going to make them both too angry to be rational. She took a deep breath and forced back all the things she wanted to say.

"When are you going?" she said as calmly as she could.

"Monday." He glanced at her and then away. "We'll fly out of Seattle to the Philippines and go down from there."

Her heart was breaking. "How long will you be gone?"

"Not too long. Two weeks at the most."

"Or forever."

He turned to look at her. "Sara…" Reaching out, he grabbed her hand and held it tightly, as though he might be able to convince her by touch.

"What makes you think you can succeed?" she asked him fiercely. She pulled his hand up to press it to her cheek, looking at him with all her agony plain to see in her eyes. "Why can't you just notify the authorities in that place? Why can't someone in an official capacity take care of it?"

He appeared pained. "See, Sara, you don't understand how things work in places like that. There is no official authority taking care of civil rules and regulations. Everyone's being paid off by someone. The only rule is the rule of gold. Rich people get their way, the others scrabble to stay alive. Regular Joes don't have a chance."

"But then why…?"

"Unless they get together and form a unit, like the guys and I are planning to do."

She shook her head. Tears flooded her eyes. "Jake, you said it felt like you'd stepped into civilized behavior by moving in here. Can't you understand that part of civilized behavior is having an authority force that can keep the order and make sure bad things don't happen? When people take the law into their own hands, society falls apart."

He nodded solemnly. "I hear your words and I understand what you're saying. I even agree with what you're saying." His gaze rose to meet hers. "But then I come back to what my heart tells me to do, and my heart says, go." He shrugged as though he knew there was no way he could make her understand.

"These are my friends, my fellow soldiers, and I owe them my allegiance. Some of my buddies are still in that prison camp. We can't leave them there. We have to rescue them."

She took a shuddering breath and dropped his hand, pulling away. "If you go, if you do this thing, I'll never forgive you."

He watched her. He saw the fire in her eyes and he knew the threat behind it. A dark, burning anger simmered in him that she would be thinking that way, but he knew that she was—and he thought he had some idea why. After all, marrying him hadn't been her first choice.

He knew what he was risking. He'd wondered about it ever since he'd heard about the three-month grace period during which

Sara could file a complaint against him. She'd wanted Savannah all for herself from the beginning. If she could get Savannah without him attached, she would probably like it better that way, even now.

"What are you going to do, Sara? File a grievance with the agency? File a lawsuit to get me disqualified?"

She stared at him, stung that he would think such a thing, but she didn't answer.

Suddenly his eyes filled with fury. "So that's it. You've been hoping for something like this, haven't you?" He rose and started to leave the room. "Well, here you go. Have at it. See you in court." And he was gone.

Sara sat in shock. How had it come to this? How could he think that she was just waiting for an excuse to catch him out? Didn't he understand how she felt about him?

Obviously not.

He barely looked at her the next day and didn't speak to her at all. She was in misery, but she didn't know how to approach him. She couldn't weaken on the trip. She couldn't give him her permission to go. And yet, what did she have if he left this way? She had to find a way to talk him out of it.

She found out where Starman was staying. Leaving Savannah with Jill, she took the ferry to the mainland and found the rented room, knocking on the door. A very surprised and startled Starman opened it to her, and she surprised him even more by insisting she wanted to come in.

"I have to talk to you," she told him. "I know about the mission you guys are planning to the prison camp."

Starman scowled. "Jake shouldn't have told you about that."

"You're the one who gave me the alert," she noted. "And I've talked to Jake. And now I want to ask a favor of you. Please, please convince him that he can't go."

He looked shocked at the thought. "But, Sara, he's our best man. Without him, the entire mission will fail."

"No, it won't." She wished she knew how to be more persuasive. "You can keep it on an even keel. You've been his right hand man all along. You can do it."

Starman thought for a minute, then nodded.

"You're right," he said. "I can do it. But do I want to do it without Jake?"

"I don't know. Do you?"

"No." He scowled at her. "No, I don't." He glared at her for a moment, then added grudgingly, "But I will."

She nodded, smiling in relief. "Good. Because, Starman, you know he's done it before. He's done his part. He's never shirked, has he? It's just that his circumstances have changed. He can't go do this sort of thing anymore."

Starman didn't look happy about it. "I guess you're right."

"Yes. Now here's the hard part. You have to talk him out of going."

He frowned, shaking his head. "But I just talked him *into* going."

She shrugged, tugging nervously on the buttons of her sweater, one after another. "Tell him you've changed your mind."

He looked confused. "But I haven't."

"No. But I have. I don't want him to go."

"Oh. Right."

"He's got a baby now. He's got me. He can't act like a footloose adventurer. He needs to be here, building a life, building a business, finding ways to make this all work. The prison camp should be in his past, not his future. Can't you explain that to him?"

"Sure." He straightened his shoulders and looked tough. "I can do that." He wavered for a moment. "Doesn't mean he'll listen."

"I know. But you can try."

He nodded, looking emotional. "You know I'd do just about anything for you and that little girl. Okay. I'll try."

And he did.

But it didn't do any good. Jake came to her right away to tell her that Starman had failed.

"Listen, Sara," he said, holding her hand. He didn't want to get into a fight if he could help it. "I know you mean well, but you can't get to me through my friends. It won't work."

She shrugged, searching his beautiful face, wishing she knew the right words. "I had to try," she said softly. "Oh, Jake, I'm so scared."

He looked at her in surprise. Her eyes were huge and filling with tears. He wanted to pull her close, but he hesitated.

"I wish I could make you understand," he said. "It's a matter of honor. It's a matter of loyalty and camaraderie. They need me.

I'm there for them if I possibly can be. I owe them that. We've got to go. We've all got to go. We've got to make those bastards pay for what they did to us and rescue those we left behind."

She shook her head, tears coming fast. "I think I do understand. Being a rescuer is part of who you are, and you don't want to lose that part of your identity. But, Jake—you have a new role now. You're a father. And for the next few years, that has to come first."

She was right, and yet… He couldn't do it. He couldn't turn his back on his friends. He reached down to kiss her and her arms came around his neck, pulling tightly.

A shiver went through him. He realized that he was risking more than losing Savannah. He was risking losing Sara, too, and that was becoming more and more important to him. For just a moment, he wavered.

But Jake left on Monday, just as he'd planned. She was still totally against it and she didn't let up, but she kissed him goodbye and wished him luck, and then stood with Savannah in her arms as he drove off toward the ferry. He looked back and saw her and everything in him wanted to turn around and go back. But he couldn't do that.

Sara went on, living the next few days just the way she had been doing for the last two months. But she felt like a robot. No emotion. No joy. Everything she did was under a cloud of doom. She was sure something terrible was going to happen.

Mrs. Truesdale called to check on how things were going and Sara tried to put on a calm front. Unfortunately the woman saw right through it.

"All right, Sara. Tell me what's happened. I can tell there's a problem. Let me help."

There was no way Sara was going to tell her where Jake was or what he was doing, but she couldn't hide the unhappiness, no matter how cheerful she tried to appear.

Mrs. Truesdale could smell out dissension in the ranks. "My dear, whatever it is you're going through, believe me, I'm on your side. We've been through a lot together in getting this situation squared away, and I was so sorry things seemed to be ruined when Jake appeared out of nowhere. I made sure you two had the grace period in your contract, just in case. And if you find that you need to exercise that clause, you call me right away. I'll do all I can for you."

"Oh, but there's really nothing wrong...."

"Just remember, you have a duty to that little girl. You are the gatekeeper for her future welfare. If you feel something is going awry, you must take action."

Sara hung up the phone feeling worse than before she'd talked to the woman. Jake had accused her of wanting to use the grace period clause when he'd been angry with her, but she'd never even imagined doing such a thing. No. Jake was Savannah's father. She couldn't take that away from her—or him. Jake was who he was, and no matter how angry she got with him, she would never betray him. Didn't he know that?

She packed Savannah up and headed for Jill's house, hoping to get some reassurance and moral support, but Jill was in a frenzy over a last minute order for her Bundt cakes and Sara kept her misery to herself. Jill had enough to contend with.

She took her baby home and watched her

play as she fixed her dinner. She watched the international news, in case there was anything on about the Pacific area, but nothing out of the ordinary seemed to be happening. She turned off the TV and started to gather the plates. For just a second, she happened to look up, and there was Savannah, taking her first step.

She clamped her hands over her mouth to stop the scream that wanted to alert the world, and then she laughed and ran to her girl, helping her back up when she fell, and coaxing her to do it again.

"Wow," she said. "Barely more than ten months and a half and you're walking! If only…" Her voice choked and tears filled her eyes. Jake should have been there to see this. How could he miss a milestone like this? It wasn't right.

Suddenly she was angry. Her tears melted away. What good were they, anyway? This was all Jake's doing and he was paying the price.

But so was Savannah! It wasn't fair. Her daddy ought to be there for her special achievements. It made her so angry that he'd voluntarily walked out on that.

She put Savannah down for the night and then went out to sit in the living room. She left the lamp off so she could see the lights across the bay. Should she consider doing what Mrs. Truesdale obviously thought she should—file a complaint against Jake? Did Savannah deserve it? Did Jake?

She wasn't sure. She didn't want to. But if he was off doing what he felt was his duty, maybe she ought to be doing the same. She looked at her phone and tried to decide. She knew she could call Mrs. Truesdale's number and get her answering machine. All it would take was a couple of words, and the gears would begin to grind.

Was she really that angry with Jake?

She closed her eyes. She couldn't do it. With a sigh, she got up and went to bed.

It must have been about three in the morning when she woke up and realized there was a man in her room. She wanted to scream but he was already sliding onto the bed to sit beside her. Leaning down, he whispered in her ear.

"It's me, Sara. It's Jake."

She gasped, trying to shake the cobwebs from her sleepy brain. "What?" she said, then lowered her voice, thinking of Savannah. "Jake! How did you get here?"

"I flew into Seattle a few hours ago. I didn't want to call and wake you up."

"Jake…" She reached for him. "Oh, Jake. You're safe. You're back." Clinging to him, she burst into sobs.

He held her, but his voice was full of surprise. "Sara, what's the matter? Are you okay?"

She sobbed harder, rocking the bed with it.

"Why are you crying? There isn't anything wrong with Savannah, is there?"

She shook her head. Finally she managed to get a word out.

"Oh, Jake, you didn't die."

He thought about that for a few seconds, then asked, incredulous, "Do you really care that much?"

She only pressed against him harder, her face buried in his chest, her fingers clutching at his muscular arms. He was back. Those words kept echoing in her head. He was back. He wasn't out in a jungle waiting to be killed.

The relief she felt proved how utterly shell-shocked she'd been by his going.

He stroked her hair and murmured sweet words and finally she pulled back, hiccupped and sniffed deeply. "You jerk!" she cried at him. "You claim to know all about the nuances of women's emotions. Hah!"

He looked bewildered. "When did I ever claim that?"

"Numerous times." She sniffed again, feeling around for a handkerchief. He provided one. "If you're so good at it, how come you can't even tell if your own wife loves you? Huh?"

He drew back, astonished. "Seriously?"

"You!" She threw a pillow at him. "Yes, seriously. I completely love you and you…you…"

"Wow." He stared at her in wonder. "Who knew?"

"Anyone with half a brain," she muttered, using the handkerchief and handing it back. Then she stared at him in the darkness. "Is it over? Did you do what you went to do?"

He pulled her back into his arms. "No. I only made it as far as Hawaii. We met there and I decided to come home."

Home. It had a good sound. So he considered this place home, did he? She felt a glow beginning in her heart.

"And the others?"

"They went on. They're prepared and well-equipped. And I decided I had more important things to do at home."

That word again! It was like gold to her.

"I talked to Starman. He set me straight. Sort of slapped me around and told me to wake up." He grinned. "Figuratively speaking, of course."

"Of course."

"I've been on these missions before. I'm usually one of the ones saying we've got to do it. But there was something missing. I began to realize it wasn't fair to you, or to Savannah. And that was when I decided I could use money instead of flesh and blood. The more money they have, the less chance something will go horribly wrong."

"Oh." She tried to understand, but her mind was fuzzy. She only knew that he was here with her and not over there and that was all that mattered right now.

"Well, nowadays, I've got money," he reminded her. "I can do my part that way, funding the guys and making sure they have all the supplies they need. Giving them a little bribe money to grease a few palms and make sure they don't get held up for ransom. Things like that."

"A financial backer," she said sleepily. "A philanthropist."

"Maybe. I was torn, Sara. But now I'm not. I know what is most important to me. It's you, you and Savannah. It's home. That's where I have to be."

She sighed with happiness, stretching next to him. He kissed her mouth and she sighed again.

"I love you, Sara," he said, his voice husky with emotion. "I realized that while I was in Hawaii, missing you and your warm smile. I love you like I never thought I could love a woman. You taught me how."

"I feel the same way," she said with a sigh. "I was never going to love a man, and then there was you."

His kiss was deep and hot and had all the sparkle she would ever need.

"How's Savannah?" he asked her, pulling

back to look at her in the golden lamplight. "I stopped in and looked at her on my way here. She was sleeping like a rock."

She smiled, then giggled as she remembered their baby taking her first steps. "She's fine. She's going to have a surprise for you in the morning."

"Is she?" There was a smile in his voice, too. "I can hardly wait."

"Me, too." She turned to face him. His hand slipped beneath the straps on her nightgown. "How about you, Sara?" he asked softly. "Do you have a surprise for me?"

Her pulse began a wild race through her entire system. She caught her breath at his touch. "Yes, Jake. Yes, I do."

She reached up to kiss him again, but only for a moment. He began to unbutton his shirt and pull it off, then went to his belt.

"Are you inviting me into your bed?" he asked her softly.

"I'm inviting you into *our* bed."

"That is an offer I would be a fool to refuse," he said as he came to her.

She laughed and turned in his arms, letting him pull her nightgown off and then pressing herself against his naked body. She'd never felt anything more exciting. Her breasts against his hard, rounded muscles, her skin against his smoothness, his mouth on hers—this was what she'd been waiting for ever since their wedding. She lost herself in his heat and closed her eyes, living for the moment.

He was home.

* * * * *

COMING NEXT MONTH from Harlequin® Romance

AVAILABLE JULY 1, 2013

#4383 A COWBOY TO COME HOME TO

Cadence Creek Cowboys

Donna Alward

Cooper Ford will do anything to regain his best friend Melissa Stone's trust. But can he convince her that he's ready to start a family?

#4384 HOW TO MELT A FROZEN HEART

Cara Colter

Brendan Grant's heart has been in the deep freeze since his wife's death. Can Nora and her orphaned nephew defrost his defenses?

#4385 THE CATTLEMAN'S READY-MADE FAMILY

Bellaroo Creek!

Michelle Douglas

Tess Laing moves to the Outback with her niece and nephew to start a new life. Are they the key to cattleman Cameron Manning's happiness?

#4386 RANCHER TO THE RESCUE

Jennifer Faye

Meghan Finnegan flees her wedding...and runs straight into the muscled torso of ex-rodeo champion Cash Sullivan. Is he the answer to her prayers?

You can find more information on upcoming Harlequin® titles, free excerpts and more at www.Harlequin.com.

HRLPCNM0613

LARGER-PRINT BOOKS!
GET 2 FREE LARGER-PRINT NOVELS PLUS
2 FREE GIFTS!

⊞ HARLEQUIN®

Romance

From the Heart, For the Heart

HRLP13R

HARLEQUIN® *Romance*

Grab your Stetson and put on your cowboy boots because July at Harlequin Romance is all about gorgeous cowboys and everything Western!

Travel with us from the Rocky Mountains to New Mexico, from Western Canada to the Australian Outback and watch as our four plucky heroines lasso their very own hero.

Find out in…

Donna Alward—*A Cowboy To Come Home To*

Cara Colter—*How to Melt a Frozen Heart*

Michelle Douglas—*The Cattleman's Ready-Made Family*

And introducing **Jennifer Faye** with *Rancher to the Rescue!*

An unforgettable collection!

Available wherever books and ebooks are sold.